Mystery of the Fog Man

AN AVON  CAMELOT BOOK

Mystery of the Fog Man

by Carol Farley

Illustrated by Joseph Escourido

To the memory
of the dreams
we dreamed on
Melendy Street

6th grade reading level has been determined by using the Fry
Readability Scale.

AVON BOOKS
A division of
The Hearst Corporation
959 Eighth Avenue
New York, New York 10019

Copyright © 1966 by Carol J. Farley
Published by arrangement with the author
Library of Congress Catalog Card Number: 82-13900
ISBN: 0-380-00102-0

Library of Congress Cataloging in Publication Data

Farley, Carol J.
   Mystery of the fog man.

   (An Avon/Camelot book)
   Summary: Thirteen-year-olds Larry and Kip have
their hands full untangling the mysterious sudden
appearances and disappearances of the Fog Man
and solving the theft of a large sum of money from
the ferry Wolverine.
   [1. Mystery and detective stories.   2. Crime and
criminals—Fiction]   I. Excourido. Joseph, ill.
II. Title.
PZ7.F233My   1974   [Fic]   82-13900
ISBN 0-380-00102-0

First Camelot Printing, November, 1974

BAN   10 9 8 7 6

MYSTERY OF THE FOG MAN

CHAPTER ONE

I can't stop thinking about what happened in Ludington the summer I was thirteen. When I least expect it, I suddenly find myself sinking into the familiar nightmare, the queer, jumbled past, where the passage of time has only magnified my memories. It's strange how clear they are. I thought that they would dim in time, that they would slowly shrink down in proportion until they matched other memories of other summers. But they haven't. They only seem to get more and more detailed. I can remember every action, every movement, every scene during the first four days I spent in Michigan. It's like watching a rerun of a horror movie on television, only it's worse, because I know that the film is in my mind and it cannot be shut off by the flick of a button. I remember everything, everyone . . . but only the fog man haunts me.

He flits through my memories the way a crack keeps appearing in an old film on the television screen. He's in every scene, in the back of every picture. I keep telling myself that he'll never be alive again, but the words sound hollow. How can he be gone if he's still so alive in my memory? How can I forget him when I see his face even in my dreams? His image is clearer in my mind than the memory of my own face in a mirror.

How well I remember the first time I saw him! I can still see the misty fog, hear the wailing foghorn, and feel the wet sand on the beach at Ludington. I had been waiting there for my cousin, standing alone, staring out at Lake Michigan. Larry and I had awakened before dawn that morning and we had decided that I should celebrate my first day in Michigan by fishing off the breakwater that served as a guide for ships coming into Ludington's harbor.

We had walked to the lake together, but Larry had stopped to see if the bait shop on the beach was open, while I, anxious for my first look at the lake, had hurried to the water's edge. There I stood, like a foreign substance washed ashore, trying to see through the fog, trying to see to the end of the huge cement wall that stretched out into Lake Michigan like a long gray arm. But I saw nothing. I only heard the eerie sound coming from the foghorn at the end of the wall, for the swirling mist blotted everything from sight.

Then suddenly I felt someone near. I still don't know how I sensed him. I couldn't have seen him, couldn't have heard his steps, yet I knew someone was there. I slowly turned and looked up the empty beach. Faintly I could make out the figure of a man shuffling through the sand. I stood without moving, almost hypnotized by the mournful foghorn blowing in the distance, while the figure limped nearer to me. He seemed to pause, to stiffen, and then the fog swirled in. I strained my eyes, trying to see in the early dawn, trying to see through the mist. As I stared, the fog drifted away and I saw him completely. I couldn't stop staring, yet I felt sickened by what I saw.

He seemed old, unbelievably old. He shuffled toward me, his beard blowing in the wind like a white flag at half-mast, for he was so crippled that his body was bent almost in two. He wore a brown overcoat that was dragging on the sand and a brown hat that almost completely covered his face. His arms were held tightly against himself, clutching his ragged coat to his body.

I stood and watched him limp through the mist, unable to talk, unable to move. I felt as though I

3

were a trespasser caught in a forbidden place, whereas he seemed to belong to the half darkness. At last the figure reached the wall that divided us, and he began to lift himself awkwardly onto it. He slowly rose to his feet again, limped across the top, and gradually lowered himself down the two feet to the harbor beach where I stood. He was so near that I could have touched him, so close that I could see the ragged cuff on his coat. Motionless, I waited for him to turn on me. To . . . to do what? I don't know what I thought he would do.

But he did nothing. He shuffled past me, his head bent over, his eyes seeing only his feet, his back curved round like a huge brown spider. Before I could stop myself, I stepped back. My throat was so tight that I could hardly breathe. Then, almost as fast as he had appeared, the old man was gone. The fog had swallowed him and I stood staring at an empty beach.

"Kipper! The bait shop is open!"

I nearly lost my balance, I whirled around so fast. "It's only me," Larry said, laughing. He jumped off the wall to the sand where I stood.

For a few seconds I just looked at him, almost expecting him to have changed since I had had my weird sensations. But he was the same—redheaded and freckled, with green eyes that slightly squinted. I felt almost hollow as the fear slowly drained from my body.

I tried to seem natural as I looked at Larry. Already, after only one night of really knowing him, I had realized how different we were. I had seen from pictures that we did not look alike: he was tall, lanky, and light-skinned; I was short, dark-haired, and always tanned. But now I knew that it was more than physical appearance that separated us. In ways I felt much younger than Larry, even though he was only a few months older. He seemed to be so sure of himself, so eager to try new things. I was always unsure, even shy. I had liked him right away, but I was afraid that he was disappointed in me. Perhaps to him I was just a boring country cousin he had to have around for a few days.

He was smiling when he jumped from the wall to the beach, but his smile disappeared when he saw me. I could feel how tight my face was, and I knew that my eyes showed my strange feelings. I was ashamed to meet his gaze, for I was sure he would see that I had been afraid; and how could I explain my strange fear to someone like Larry?

He took my arm. "What happened down here, Kipper? You look like you saw a ghost."

I swallowed loudly and kicked the sand with my foot. "I saw a man," I finally began, knowing how foolish it would sound, "with the funniest outf——"

"Brown coat? Beard? Limping?"

"You know him?"

Larry leaned against the breakwater and folded his arms. "Well, now you've really been welcomed to

5

Ludington," he said. "You've just met the fog man. He's our biggest tourist attraction."

"The fog man!"

Larry laughed. "That's not his real name, Kip. Nobody knows that. He's just a funny old guy who walks around the beaches here. Someone once called him the fog man and now everyone does."

"But who is he really? What's he doing here?" I tried to fit the old man into the mental picture that I had formed of Ludington. Even though the city seemed large to me, I knew it was small and closely knit. The whole area was isolated in its surroundings: Lake Michigan faced it on the west and north; and large forests bounded it on the east and south. It seemed impossible that a stranger could live there and not be known, and I knew I'd never be satisfied until I found out more about him. "Are you sure you don't know who he really is?" I asked again.

Larry answered slowly, looking at me with a puzzled frown. "I'm telling you, Kipper, nobody knows anything about this guy."

"But you must know," I said. "You wrote me that everybody knows everything about everybody in this town."

"Everybody but him," Larry answered. "He's been coming around here for more than three years, but we still don't know any more about him now than we did the first day he walked in from the woods. He combs the beaches all summer, then he disappears. Nobody knows where he really comes from or where he goes during the winter. But nobody thinks much about it anymore. He's like the foghorn—we hear it so often that we don't hear it at all. We see him so much that we don't even notice him. He's just part of the beach in summertime."

"But what's he doing here?" I asked, sensing even as I spoke that Larry had heard enough of my questions.

"He picks up driftwood—that's why he walks up and down the beach, I guess. When he finds a good piece, he sells it to Miss Norton in the gift shop up by the road. She gives him money for the food that he buys. He doesn't wear anything but that brown outfit, so he doesn't need money for clothes. We think he lives back in the woods someplace."

"Doesn't anybody ever ask him?"

"He can't talk. Miss Norton says she thinks that he's a deaf-mute."

"And crippled, too," I added.

"Well, he won't let anybody help him. Even Dad tried. The fog man always tries to run when anybody gets near him, but he nearly flew when he saw Dad in his police uniform. It seemed more cruel to frighten him than it was to leave him alone. Dad decided that as long as he didn't bother anyone, there wasn't any need to bother him. We just let him go his way. The tourists try to get to him in the summer, but he's gone before most of them get up in the morning. They think it's great to buy a piece of wood that he's found."

I shaded my eyes against the rising sun and looked at the treetops all along the sand dunes to the east. "You think he lives up in that forest?"

"Could be. Hardly anybody goes deep into the woods around here. Hunting isn't much good and the camping area is near the highway. Hey, maybe we can camp out a night while you're here, huh?"

"It sure looks like a lot of forest," I said, trying to join Larry in a change of subject, even though I really wanted to ask more questions about the old man.

"You've probably got lots more out where you come from," Larry said. We were quiet a moment, then he added, "I'm sure glad you got a chance to visit—it was hard to write letters to someone I'd never seen. Sometimes I wish Dad would move back to a farm like yours." He lowered his voice. "I hope you'll like it here, Kip."

I could feel myself blush. I wanted to tell him that I was glad I had finally met him too; wanted to tell him that he had more than lived up to the image I had given him in our years of writing, but I could say nothing. When I feel anything deeply, I can never say it. "It'll be fun here," I finally blurted.

Larry seemed to sense my embarrassment. He smiled and pointed out past the breakwater. "There's something you'll have to get a closer look at. The *Wolverine*'s coming into port."

I followed his finger and through the mist I saw the bulk of a large car ferry sailing into the harbor on

8

our left. ...
traveled bet...
that one was ...
bigger than I ha...
cars from the railr...
and passengers, so I ...
they would be. We wat...
past the wall and disappea...
dock.

"Come on, now," Larry sai...
from sight. "We'll have to go up ... for
our bait. The owner opened his shop ... ay, and
if we hurry, we can be the first ones on ... wall."

We ran up the hill to the bait house. It stood at the
top of the sandbank near the beach parking lot, fac-
ing a small gift shop. I began talking about fishing
while we ran, but I was really thinking about the
creature Larry had called the fog man, and I was
only talking to cover up my thoughts. By then I had
realized that the thought of him in my brain was like
a speck of sand in my eye—perhaps it seemed huge
and uncomfortable only to me.

It took us fifteen minutes at the bait house, because
the man selling the bait started to tell me stories
about Ludington, beginning way back in its early
lumbering days. He told his stories so smoothly that I
knew he must have repeated them hundreds of times.
I've often wondered since then whether it would
have mattered if we had left right away, for his tales
didn't really mean much to me. Sometimes a few

ssly spent when you
future. If we'd been on the
few minutes maybe we . . . but I
waste of time to think about that now.
the time we left, the fog had completely
cleared. We walked slowly, watching our buckets of
minnows. It was beginning to feel warmer and everything was silent. Then, without warning, the whole
world seemed to fall apart around me. I dropped my
bucket. Larry stopped with one foot still in the air. A
whistle so high and so shrill was blowing so loudly
that I thought my eardrums would break.

"What's that?" I shouted. "What's that, Larry?"

"The car ferry!" Larry dropped his bucket, turned,
and started to run down the beach. "Something's
happened at the dock!"

The piercing wail came again, even louder, and I
recognized the whistle of a car ferry being used as an
emergency alarm. I turned and ran behind Larry,
kicking sand as I went. We raced down the beach
path around the bend to the dock. The loud wailing
blotted out everything in my mind, and as proof that
strong emotion kills reason, I felt fear take control of
my body. I followed Larry blindly.

CHAPTER TWO

It's strange how fast people flock together when there's trouble. The beach had seemed deserted only moments before, yet as soon as that alarm sounded, people came running out from everywhere. I wonder whether persons gather at disasters because they feel that by being there they sort of gain immunity from the same thing happening to them . . . it's queer. I have to admit, though, that Larry and I were just like everybody else. We turned off the beach and ran up into the shipyard area right along with all the others.

"It's the *Wolverine*'s whistle!" Larry shouted.

We came to a dead stop. A barricade blocked the road that led directly to the boat docks, and a crowd of people were being held there. We could see the *Wolverine* in dock. The men and women on the boat were holding their ears while the whistle shrieked. The shipyard swarmed with men running between the ticket office and the ship.

Suddenly the whistle stopped, and it almost seemed as though the people stopped momentarily also—that time, as we knew it, had revolved around the shrieking whistle. Then everyone was shouting and running again.

A large man in faded overalls stood near the barricade. "Sorry," he shouted almost gleefully, "nobody can get in here and nobody can get out! The yards are completely blockaded."

"What's happened?" "What's going on?" "Anybody hurt?" The crowd seemed to become one huge shouting mass.

Looking pleased, the guard threw out his chest and began telling the story. "Someone stole thirty thousand dollars from the *Wolverine*!" he shouted to everyone. "They were bringing the money from Kewaunee in the ship's safe. When they docked, the safe was empty."

"How?" "Who did it?" The crowd surged against us as Larry began dragging me forward.

"Can we get in?" he asked. "I have to see my dad."

Frowning, the guard turned from his fascinated audience, recognized Larry, looked uncertain, and then nodded. "It's okay, I guess." He called across to the other guard, "It's Chief Levitt's boy." Then he turned back to his increasing number of charges. "It was a robbery!" he shouted happily to the newcomers.

Larry and I crawled beneath the barricade, thanked the unhearing sentry, and ran toward the nearest building. "Sometimes it pays to have a father who's Chief of Police," Larry panted beside me. "That's Dad's car over there." He pointed to a black car parked beside the ticket office. "He must be inside."

The door was open; we saw Uncle Matt standing at the far window staring out at the shipyard. He turned when we ran up the steps. "I see you broke through the blockade," he said. "Someday people are going to get wise and realize you're not really necessary, my boy." He smiled and winked at me. "Larry usually gets to the scene of a crime before the criminal has a chance to leave. Were you fishing?"

I only shook my head. It was hard to remember that the tall, important-looking police chief was the same balding, middle-aged uncle I had met the night before.

"We didn't even get our lines in the water," Larry said. "And it looks like we won't now either. That whistle probably scared all the fish clear to Wisconsin. What's up?"

"Just what they're saying out there." Uncle Matt pointed through the window where we could see the crowd, growing even larger, still swarming around the men at the barricade. "Somebody cleaned out the *Wolverine*'s safe, bag and all. The safe is still unlocked, so it looks like someone had a key, unlocked it as the ship docked, grabbed the waterproof bag of money, and left in a big hurry."

Larry whistled. "A key! And the safe was left unguarded when they had that much money? Wasn't that pretty careless?"

Uncle Matt ran his hand over his right eye. "We can say it looks careless now, but that's because of the robbery. Lots of things seem pretty sensible until it's too late for it to matter anymore. The officials had a guard in there during the trip over, but he helps to lay the gangplank when the ship docks, so he left his post. In the few minutes that he was gone, someone slipped in, unlocked the safe, took the money, shut the door again, and left. The guard thought the safe was still locked, so no one knew about the robbery until the safe was opened."

"But how could anybody get the key?" Larry asked. He leaned against a desk, while I stood awkwardly shifting from one foot to the other.

"It's an old safe—the lock is unusual. We figure that one of the workers in that area got hold of the key for a few minutes one time—long enough to make a wax impression—then had a key made. He waited until the time was ripe, took a chance on what was in the safe, opened it, cleaned it out, and beat it. He was lucky. Nobody but officials of the railway know when that much money comes through. This guy got a bigger haul than he could have dreamed of."

"What are the chances of catching him?"

"The dock's closed off and we're making a complete search. We know that all of the passengers are still in the yards and we're searching their baggage and packages. The whistle called the crew together, so we'll soon know where they all are. My men are making a complete search of the ship. Whoever pulled off this job knows the ship pretty well, but a bag of money is hard to hide. Personally, I think we'll find both the thief and the missing bag right here."

"What if you don't?" I asked.

Uncle Matt almost smiled. "Then we'll find them wherever they are. Ludington is locked up tighter than a drum and has been since the alarm sounded. Nobody could have reached the city limits before my squad cars did. That means that neither the thief nor the money can possibly get out of the city. There are only two roads leading from here and they both are guarded—all vehicles will be searched. The Coast Guard is watching all the small craft that leave the shoreline. Nobody can get away from this area without being thoroughly searched."

Uncle Matt stopped talking, bent down, and leaned on the desk. "I'll tell you this, boys," he said. "Whoever took that money is stuck. Stuck right here in this area." He smiled. "And better yet—the money is stuck here, too."

"Can you really check everybody?" I asked.

Larry laughed. "Christopher thinks he's in a big city, Dad."

They have different problems in cities," Uncle Matt said. "Around here we can take care of every exit. We have men po——"

Someone stamped at the door, and a short man with a figure like the fellow they use in those weight-lifting ads came barging in. His uniform was black and gold, and even though it bulged at the waist it looked official. He frowned at Larry and me, then looked at Uncle Matt. "You were right," he said slowly. "Two men—Arnold Johanson and George Karminsky—are missing." He shook his head and lowered himself into the chair by the desk. "I can't believe it. Karminsky I hardly know—he's a new worker, been with me only a few trips. But Arnold! I've known him for years. He's been with me ever since I became captain on the *Wolverine*. He couldn't be in on anything like this."

"Have you checked everywhere he might have gone?"

"Everywhere." The captain looked mournful and shook his head again. He looked off, gazing at a spot above my head. Then his head jerked and he smiled. "Fishing! That's it! Sometimes Arnold goes fishing when we dock and he isn't on duty. He's got a rowboat tied up just outside the ships' docks. He must have gone today. We'd been docked almost five minutes before we sounded the alarm. Arnold could have been off and gone in his rowboat before he knew what happened. He could be on his way back right now!"

As if on cue, steps thundered on the porch. "Captain Moore!" Another man, as tall and thin as the captain was short and stocky, came running in. "Arnold's back. He heard the whistle when he was out in the water with his boat. He stood up to see what was going on and tipped the whole thing over, so it took him awhile to get it righted again. He's in getting dry clothes now. He says he hasn't seen Karminsky though. He saw him on board after we left Kewaunee, but he hasn't seen him since."

"I knew it!" The captain smiled, as though the crime were less serious now that he knew his personal friend was not involved. "Now that leaves only Karminsky. He must be the one. How long do you think it'll be before you pick him up?"

"We're checking now," Uncle Matt answered. "There's a lot to be done yet."

"Let's get our gear then, Kipper," Larry said. "No sense in wasting our time fishing when we could help out here." We started toward the door.

"Forget it, boys," Uncle Matt called after us. "There's lots of work to do, but there's nothing that you can help with. You two go ahead and fish for awhile. I'll see you back at the house for lunch."

Larry and I walked back up the road to the barricade. The people were still shouting at the guard, but he seemed to have lost his enthusiasm. Getting attention must be like eating potato chips: at first you don't think you'll ever have enough and then, without warning, you know you've had too much. He barely waved as we crawled under the boards.

It was a lot different walking back to the breakwater. We walked slowly, our heads down. I tried to think of something interesting to say, for I felt that Larry was disappointed. Perhaps Uncle Matt would have let him help out if I had not been there. I felt dull and gray. Then I saw an object lying on the beach.

"There's something I never even noticed when we ran past," I said. "People must really get blinded by fear—I don't remember seeing that at all." We stopped beside a large board half buried in the sand. Pieces stuck out from both sides. "What's that, Larry?"

"It's part of a ship." He bent over and brushed some of the sand off. "It washed ashore two years ago—we aren't sure what boat it came from. Lots of ships have been wrecked in Lake Michigan —it could be from any one of them. The last biggest one was in 1910. A car ferry, *P.M. No. 18*, went down north of here. Some of the bodies washed ashore; some didn't. This wreckage could be part of that ship—or even part of a schooner that went down in 1900."

"Nineteen hundred? You think it could take *that* long to wash ashore?" I bent over to look more closely. The wood was gray and pitted, like lumber that's been underwater a long time.

Larry sat on his haunches staring out at the lake. "Could take that long," he said. "People don't know everything there is to know about Lake Michigan. Lots of scientists think there's a giant whirlpool deep underwater, way out past the coast of Illinois. I guess if there is one moving continuously about and some-thing gets going around in it, it could take years and years to surface again."

"A whirlpool!" I exclaimed. I stood and stared out at the calm, soothing water again. "It's hard to believe."

"Well, nobody knows for sure," Larry answered. He looked up the beach, then stood still. "There's something else we missed," he said, pointing ahead.

We ran a few yards through the warm sand. A green rowboat, wet inside and only half out of the water, stood near the path we had followed down the shoreline when we had run to the docks.

"Must be that fellow's boat," Larry said. "Looks like it was tipped over all right."

We looked inside and saw both oars and two life preservers. "Wonder if he lost his fishing stuff," I remarked. "There isn't any here."

"Probably carried it back to shore with him," Larry told me. "I don't see anything floating in the water. Funny we didn't notice him when we ran past."

We pulled the boat all the way up on the beach and walked on to our poles and buckets. The breakwater was still deserted, but cars were pulling up in the parking lot near the road. I looked at my watch. "It's only nine o'clock," I said. "Things have happened too fast this morning. I thought it must be nearly noon."

Larry laughed. "Things aren't usually this jumping," he said. "Ludington can get pretty dull. Guess our excitement is over for today though. Nothing much more can hap——"

He never got to finish his sentence. A tall, brown-haired woman was running down from the main road. "Boys!" she screamed, her voice as shrill as the whistle had been. "Boys! You've got to help me!"

20

CHAPTER THREE

She ran in that funny, knock-kneed way that some girls do, her legs going to the sides, kicking up sand to the right and the left. In the fraction of a second that I stood there just staring, I saw that she was tall, thin, with her hair in braids which were wrapped around her head. Then Larry grabbed my arm. "Don't pay any attention," he whispered cryptically. Before I could turn to him, the woman was beside us.

"Larry!" she shouted into our faces. "Thank heaven you're here!" Before either of us could answer, she rushed on. "You know that awful robbery?" She paused a second, like a basketball poised in flight on the basket rim; then she blurted, "The robber is right up there in my store! I heard the whistle blowing, so I ran out with everybody else and I left my shop door open. I ran up the road to hear what happened and I just now came back. The door was closed! I know I left it open. That man must have gone inside. I'm sure he's hiding in there right now!"

Larry nodded slowly. "You don't think that the wind blew it shut, Miss Norton?"

"No!" The woman spoke the word before Larry finished the question. Her eyes almost popped out of her head. I stood silent, letting Larry handle everything. His whispered warning made me hesitate to speak at all.

"We'll go up and see about it," he said. "Wait here —we'll come down when we're through looking inside the shop."

"Be careful," she told us, speaking almost in a whisper. "He may have a gun. Robbers usually do, you know." I would have wondered more about how she knew so much about robbers, but I was thinking instead of the way she was speaking. Her whisper was much louder than her normal speaking voice, but she seemed to feel compelled to whisper anyway. She sort of folded up against the breakwall as we started toward the gift shop.

"Do you think we should go in alone?" I asked Larry.

He laughed out loud. "Nobody's in that store!" he said. "You can bet on it."

I almost stopped walking. "How do you know? She just now told us that——"

"She's told a lot of people a lot of things!" Larry spoke louder now that we were almost to the door. "Miss Norton is always finding somebody hiding somewhere. I can't tell you how many times Dad has hurried over to her house in the middle of the night. She's always hearing noises, always seeing shadows, always sensing danger. She's scared of her own shadow!"

We reached her store and Larry opened the glass door. "Come on in," he said. "You might as well look around—she won't come up until we make a long search."

A bell rang when we closed the door. I stared at the inside. Miss Norton seemed to have imagination all right. She had more stuff crammed into that little store than you or I or anybody else could ever have imagined. Even the ceiling was covered with a fishnet that was stuffed with painted shells and colored beads. There wasn't room for a rooster to hide in there—let alone a robber.

"She's alone most of the time," Larry said. "That's probably why she gets so scared. Sure makes it hard on Dad though. It almost kills him to get up in the middle of the night for no real reason."

I turned to a table near the window. It was the least crowded of any of the displays and it seemed to be the most expensive. There were six pieces of driftwood on a green satin cloth. I looked at the price tags.

"Wow!" I said. "Seems like there's more than one robber around here. Look at the price she's asking for a piece of wood."

"Those are the fog man specials, Kip." Larry came over and pointed out a small white paper. "Miss Norton has written here the story of the old guy who prowls the beaches looking for this wood. The resorters eat it up! They buy this stuff just because of the story, I guess, because it really isn't any different from the wood they can pick up themselves."

I suddenly remembered my encounter with the old man in the fog and felt my hands grow cold. "It's a mystery to me," Larry was saying, "how Miss Norton can stand to be alone with that old guy. She's scared to death of most people and he even gives me the creeps. Course, I guess the money from the wood helps her out a lot."

I moved away from the driftwood. "Let's go," I said, forcing myself to forget the lonely brown figure. Just being near the things I knew he had handled made me feel tight inside.

We walked back to Miss Norton. She was still leaning on the breakwall, but her eyes fit in her head again. "He wasn't there?" she whispered.

"All safe," Larry answered. He picked up our fishing gear. "We'll be out on the wall in case you need us," he said. "But I don't think you'll have any trouble. I have a hunch that the thief is probably a long way from here by now."

"I hope so. I'm all alone in that shop, you know—

24

anything could happen. People forget that I'm even——" We heard her still mumbling as she walked through the sand back to her shop.

Neither of us had any luck fishing. We sat out on the breakwall near the lighthouse at the end, then moved in nearer to the swimming area at the shoreline, but we caught nothing. Maybe the whistle really had scared all the fish away—or maybe we were just too excited to sit still long enough. Other fishermen came later in the morning; a few caught perch, but most of them didn't get anything. We finally gave up and walked toward shore with our poles.

We stopped near the swimming area by the wall. A diving board had been connected to the wall and some of the swimmers were pretty good divers. I met a few of Larry's friends, but mostly I just watched Lake Michigan. It was warm and calm and colored a deep blue. The sand was almost gold and it shimmered through the clear water covering the lake bottom. I lay on the wall in the warm sunlight, and when I listened to the sound of the loud laughter I could almost forget the queer feelings I'd had at dawn. I didn't realize then that the image of the fog man was implanted in my brain like a small seed—a seed that looks innocent enough, but one that grows and grows until it's a huge monstrous growth that blocks off everything in its path.

At lunchtime we headed back to Larry's house, just a few blocks from the lake. Because his mother had died when he was small, Larry had been making lunches most of his life. So by the time Uncle Matt arrived we had the table set with sandwiches and milk.

As soon as he walked in the door, I knew the news was bad. I had already discovered that when Uncle Matt rubbed his eyes, he was worried. Now he came in, rubbing his eyes and looking miserable.

"Not a sign of Karminsky," he told us. "I think now that he never even planned to leave this area. He would have tried to get out immediately if he intended to try at all. He hasn't even made an attempt."

"Is that so bad?" Larry asked. "If he hasn't left the area, then you know for sure that he must be nearby. That sounds like good news to me."

"I don't think so." Uncle Matt reached for a sandwich and, between bites, he told us of his suspicions. "I think the fellow planned this job a long time ago. At first I thought it was just a spur-of-the-moment robbery. Now, the more I think about it, the more I feel that he knew exactly what was in that safe. I think he waited until he saw the haul was worth his troubles. He could have checked the safe periodically with his key—if he didn't disturb anything, no one would know he had been in there."

Larry's eyes grew large. "You mean he had the key a long time?"

"Probably. It all hinges on this escape business. Since he didn't make a quick break, he must have planned all along to hide out here. If he wanted to stay around here, there'd be lots of places to hide—but he would have to have food. He would know that he couldn't buy supplies after the robbery, so he'd have to have food hidden somewhere in the woods. If he had bought the food beforehand, then he must have already planned to steal the money."

"I get it! He can hide out now, then, until the highways are no longer guarded."

"I'm afraid that's it." Uncle Matt rubbed his eyes again. "He knows we can't guard the highways forever. With tourists coming in and out of this area all summer long, we'll have to call off the searching soon. We'll have good weather for months. If it's a waiting game we're playing, I'm afraid Mr. Karminsky has the drop on us."

"He does, unless you find him first," Larry said. Then he added, "Or somebody else finds him."

Uncle Matt looked at Larry, then at me. "Don't you two start getting ideas now," he warned.

"When will you start searching the woods, Dad?"

"Not today—and neither will you. I want all the available men guarding the highways, and I want you and all your friends to stay out of this." He stood for a moment, then picked up his hat and went to the door. "Remember," he called back, "you two go down to the beach this afternoon."

When the door shut, Larry looked at me. "Feel like a search?" he asked.

I grinned. "Sure, but your father said——"

"My father said we should go to the beach, and so

we will. We'll go to the beach, then we'll go up the road and head into the woods. Okay?"

"Okay," I said.

Minutes later we were headed back toward the lake. Neither of us said so, but we both were pretty excited. And, though I never would have admitted it, I was also just a little scared. I liked the idea of the search all right, but I was just a little bit worried about what we might find.

CHAPTER FOUR

Something comes alive inside of me when I walk in the woods. I don't know how to explain it—it's a feeling that doesn't have a name. Maybe it isn't named because nobody else has ever experienced it; I don't know. All I know is that a forest gives me a feeling of peace, a sense of well being, a sureness that most of life is good. My problems seem dwarfed by the trees; my worries are silenced by the wind; my insecurities seem foolish beside the life struggle of the animals. I feel like I want to burst out of myself, want to gather all the tree branches in my arms and fly with the wind over the forest.

That day with Larry was even more special. I didn't mention my strange love for the woods because I was afraid of what Larry would think, and if I can't share an emotion I'd rather not admit having it. Even without my saying anything, though, I felt that Larry sensed my mood and the two of us walked in awed silence. We had long since left the beach where we had promised Uncle Matt we would go and we were now walking in the forest area about a mile from the main camping grounds, ready, finally, to look for definite signs made by the missing man.

Our footsteps were hushed in the stillness. The sun made queer patterns peering through the leaves. "You look spotted," Larry told me, breaking the silence. I laughed and headed for a huge oak tree.

"Let's sit awhile," I said, plopping down. "I have to rest my eyeballs—we should start looking closely now that we're this far back in the woods."

Larry lay down on the ground a few feet away. After a long silence, he spoke. "I'd like to find Karminsky."

He said the words so slowly, so clearly, that I straightened up, no longer sleepy. His voice seemed deeper, almost adult.

"You sound really serious," I said. "Like it means life or death to you."

Larry turned on his stomach and buried his head in his arms. "It's not life or death, Kip, but it does mean a lot to me. More than I can say. I'd do anything to help Dad on this case—anything."

"Have you helped him before?"

"Never. I've never helped Dad do anything."

"Yes, you have." I spoke louder now, thinking, like most people do, that volume makes speech more persuasive. "You help out a lot at home."

"That's not what I mean!" He turned on his back again and stared at the tree branches over our heads. "You couldn't understand how I feel because life is so easy for you. You have brothers, a mother, a father. Dad and I are all alone. If it weren't for me, Dad would go places, do things, see things. I've always tied him down; now I have a chance to make it up to him. If he catches Karminsky right away, it would really make him feel good. He'd be a big success with the rail company, and with the state. If he doesn't get him, he'll be just another hick cop. Don't you see? He's got to solve this case as soon as possible. I've got to help him!"

I nodded my head. What he said did make sense. The whole world loves a success; everybody gets embarrassed by failures. Successes get put on pedestals—failures are pushed under the nearest rug. I could see why solving this case could mean a lot to Uncle Matt—and why it would mean even more to Larry.

"I wish we had more to go on," I said. "Karminsky could be anywhere around here; if he's even here, that is."

"I know." Larry's voice cracked. "It seems like the more I think about it all, the less I can figure out. That guy could have hidden the money, given it to someone else, or taken it with him. He could be hidden here, be gone miles from here, or be secreted in somebody's basement. The more I know, the less I feel we'll find him."

"He could even be disguised," I said. I still don't know what made me say that. Sometimes words seem to come from my lips before they reach my brain.

"Disguised!" Larry sat up. "Leave it to you to come up with an idea like that!" He laughed for the first time since we had left the house. "Nobody could get away with a disguise in Ludington. You keep forgetting you're in a small town." He lay down and became serious again. "Course, if he isn't careful in the woods back here, he could get caught in quicksand and really disappear. That would be the end of everybody's plans."

"Quicksand!" I had visions of the stories I'd read where quicksand covered all traces of murder weapons and criminals. "Is there really quicksand in this area?"

"Has been. It comes and goes, I guess. Quicksand comes from underground springs, you know. The sand is normal—it's the watercourse that is different. When the water force comes up, it's a fountain; when it pulls down, it's quicksand."

"Has anybody ever been caught in it around here?"

"Not that I know of. We haven't had a bog for quite a while that anybody has discovered. Back here, though, there could be anything. Nobody ever explores deep in the woods."

"I've read that you can get out of it," I said. "If you can remain still, you'll soon settle with your head above the water, so you can still breathe."

"So who'll feed you?"

Larry's question felt like a slap on my face. Suddenly I saw a man caught in quicksand up to his neck, slowly starving to death. "I give up!" I said too loudly for the stillness of the forest. "This life is too much for me!"

"Not really," Larry answered, smiling. "I'm just giving you a rough time. Come on now, Cousin, up and at it! We'll start doing a little searching."

When I think about it now, I see how foolish we were. The forest was miles and miles long—at least eight miles deep—and we didn't even know what we were looking for. We had simply decided that we were gradually going to work our way back to the camping area searching the ground for footprints or other signs of a fresh trail. The soil was damp in the darkness of the forest and it showed plainly the trail that we ourselves had made. At first, I'd been afraid to put my feet down—the soil sunk an inch and I was constantly feeling that I had stepped into a quicksand bog, but I finally grew used to it. We hiked in the deep woods for hours, but had to admit that there was nothing unusual there.

We were on our way back home when we went through the old lumber camp. Larry was walking a few yards to my left and I was walking almost parallel to the main highway. Suddenly, in front of me, I saw a wooden hut. It was almost completely covered with bushes and vines, and it was half falling, but the weathered gray of the lumber could still be seen through the clearing.

"Larry!" I called in a hoarse whisper. "Come here!"

Larry ran over, followed my pointing finger, and stared at the shack.

"That looks like a good hideout," I said, still whispering. "Think Karminsky might be hiding in there?"

Larry dropped his shoulders dejectedly. "That's nothing, Kip," he said. "You got me all excited for nothing. That old shack has been there for ages. It was part of the lumber camp a long time ago. I guess it used to be a tool shed or something."

"Well, wouldn't it make a good hiding place?"

"Are you nuts?" Larry looked at me in disgust. "This is too easy. Anybody would think to look here. Anybody knows that." He turned to go.

"But you're not looking in there," I said.

He stopped, surprised. "You're right," he said. "Maybe it's so obvious here that it's the perfect place to hide. . . . Wait!"

He walked toward the hut. Only after he headed for the open door did I realize how dangerous his action was. If Karminsky really was inside, and he did have a gun——

"Kip! Kip!"

My fears were blasted by Larry's excited call. I dashed to his side and peered into the hut where he stood staring. There inside, in neat, even, planned rows, stood layers and layers of canned goods.

"It's his food!" Larry shouted. "We've found Karminsky's food!"

CHAPTER FIVE

My mouth felt dry. "If his food is here, then don't you thi——"

"He's near here too." Larry turned pale; his words came out like a recording played at low speed. We stared at each other, straining our ears to listen for sounds we expected, yet feared, to hear. There was only the wind, only the noise of the forest. Then together, as if one of us had commanded it, we turned away from the hut and hurried back to the foliage of the forest.

When we sat down, I felt my left eyelid twitching. My fingernails had dug into my palms and I hadn't felt it. I stared at Larry.

"He must have gone for water." Larry was no longer pale; his voice was low but clear. He seemed older, stronger. "We'll have to watch for him. We may be able to find where he hid the money."

My body was beginning to feel normal again. "I can't believe we've really found him," I said. "His hideout!" My fear was now turning into disbelief—a deep emotion always has to disappear by degrees, I guess.

"It's so simple!" Larry said. "He stocked this hut

ages ago—nobody ever comes out around here, and a stream is only a little distance away. He ran up the beach from the boat docks, then hurried across the road to the woods. He could live back here for months."

"Well, it's lucky for us he's gone now," I said, beginning to peer around. "I don't think we would have been much of a match for him if he had seen us."

"It was lucky all right!" Larry sat down and pointed south. "The stream is over that way. Let's wait here until he comes back. He shouldn't notice anything. The leaves don't look disturbed. We'll just lie low."

"Shouldn't we go get your father?"

"No!" Larry turned to me, his eyes narrowed. "When I tell Dad about this place, I want to tell him everything—where Karminsky is, where his food is, and most of all, where the money is. We'll wait. I'll wait all night if I have to."

There's something discouraging about waiting. It seems to me that the longer I sit and wait for something, the more depressed I get. I begin to wonder whether what I'm waiting for is really worth sitting still for so long. Sometimes the wait makes the actual event lose its appeal. I read once that anticipation is the best sensation. I guess that may be true, but you can only anticipate just so long before you become bored.

At least that's the way it was with Larry and me that day. At first, in the bushes, in the silence, in the sunlight, the wait was exciting. We jumped at every sound and dreamed great visions of how heroic we'd be when Karminsky came back. We didn't worry about danger; we didn't feel our cramped muscles or feel uncomfortable sitting on the damp ground.

Then, as it began to get dark, we began to wonder what we actually would do if Karminsky returned and found us; we began to get more and more uncomfortable. The ground felt harder, damper than it had when we first sat down; the noise of the birds seemed less and less thrilling and became more and more annoying. My legs began to hurt; I was tired of being so silent; and worst of all, I was hungry. We had been sitting for hours hidden in the thicket, staring out at the deserted hut, and the more we sat there, the more convinced I became that Karminsky would not be back.

"He should have come by now," I said finally to Larry. "The stream isn't that far away, is it?"

Larry frowned. "He'll be back—he's got to come back!" He peered around and then continued. "Besides, we're not sure he went to the stream anyway, are we? He may have several hideouts—maybe he's in another one."

"Then what's the use of waiting?" I said, angry now because I was so hungry. My boiling point has always gone down in direct proportion to my wait between meals.

"Well, some of his food is here! He's got to come back here sooner or later!"

39

I said nothing to Larry's arguments. Nothing seemed sensible to me. We sat silently for several minutes while the gloom in the sky deepened. Finally Larry shifted his position.

"Dad will have a fit unless we get home for supper," he said. "We have to go home soon, I suppose. Or at least one of us will have to."

He looked so disappointed that I forgot my anger —I couldn't help remembering how much finding Karminsky meant to him. "You go ahead then," I told him. "You can make some excuses to your father. I'll wait here. If you bring back a few sandwiches for me, I'll wait here all night with you if we have to."

Larry almost fell over in his haste to reach me. "You're all right, pal," he said, hitting my arm with his fist. He smiled at me and I had to smile too. I didn't feel nearly so miserable then.

"Here's what I'll do: I'll tell Dad that you and I have decided to camp out tonight, and I'll get a few blankets and some food. Lots of the fellows stay in the park all night—he'll think it's just another campout." Larry stood, rubbing his knees. "Sure feels good to stretch," he said. He turned to go, then turned back. "Are you su——"

"Yes," I said, not letting him finish. "I'll be fine. Just get going, will you? Bring lots of food, though; I'm so hungry I could eat a bear."

"Well, go ahead if you see one," he answered.

"You mean there really——" When I saw his grin I knew he had pulled another stunt. I guess I'll al-

40

ways be foolish enough to believe anything that someone says with a straight face. I picked up a rock and threw it at Larry's feet. "Scram!"

After Larry left, the silence was so quiet that it was loud. The birds had disappeared and I could hardly see the hut through the darkness. I tried to keep my thoughts along the right lines by concentrating on everything that had happened to me, but it hardly seemed possible to unscramble all the day's events. They were muddled together in my mind, as one picture flashed on top of another: the piercing whistle, the crowd at the dock, the captain's interview, the discovery of the boat, the excitement at the gift shop, the hike, the food in the hut. Yet even above all these flashing thoughts and under every reasoning idea was the remembrance of the fear, the revulsion, the weird sensation that I had felt when I had first seen the creature called the fog man. Thinking of him made me forget my cramped position and my empty stomach. What bothered me so much about him? Was he actually just a harmless old man?

I came from my deep concentration when I heard cautious footsteps. My hands went cold; sweat ran on my forehead. Was it the thief? Had Karminsky finally come back? And if he had, what was I going to do?

"It's me, Kipper."

Larry's whisper barely reached me, but it was enough to send me collapsing to the ground again. I like the feeling of relief best of all. It sort of floods your body with warmth.

"I got the works."

Larry appeared in the darkness, carrying two blankets and a couple of bags. "Didn't bring a flashlight," he said. "I thought it would be too dangerous." He handed me the larger bag.

"What's the news?" I said while my fingers searched the bag.

"Dad's calling the blockade off tomorrow. They're going to start searching the woods all around the docks." Larry sat down beside me and handed me a blanket. "Dad said we should have fun, but stay in the camping area, and all that kind of nonsense. They think this Karminsky is a pretty tough customer. He's been in jail in Milwaukee."

My sandwich stuck in my throat. "You didn't mention our search?"

"No—and I won't until we know more. I have a feeling that Karminsky will be back here soon."

But he wasn't. I guess I had known from the beginning that he wouldn't be. Everything would have been too easy then, and I'm just pessimistic enough to think that anything worth having has to take a while to get. Larry never gave up hope though; I dozed off several times and every time I awoke, I saw him sitting in the same position, staring straight ahead.

Just before dawn it started to rain. The sky turned into a raging waterfall and in minutes we were

soaked. "Come on," I said, picking up my blanket. "Let's get back to the house."

Larry, still sitting, said nothing.

"Come on," I said again. "We've got to get home."

Shrugging his shoulders, Larry stood and threw his wet blanket over his head. The water dripped down his face almost like tears from his eyes. I grabbed his arm and started pulling him toward the road. He was so disappointed that he seemed to be numb.

We had just reached the highway when the rain stopped as suddenly as it had started. Larry made a movement to turn back. "Let's change our clothes first," I said. "We can get dry clothes at the house and come back here later."

"Okay."

Larry's answer was hardly better than his silence. We plodded up the road without speaking. In the east the sun was slowly rising, casting a queer light on the trees and the road. A light haze hung over the forest. Larry walked along looking straight ahead; I looked to the sun, then to the lake on the west. Without realizing it, I guess I was looking for a brown, lumbering figure. The light was the same as it had been the first time I saw him, and I felt the same uneasy sensation.

Suddenly I spotted him. He was walking near the woods on the other side of the road, coming straight toward us. I knew he hadn't yet realized we were there.

"Larry!" I said, feeling that queer knotting in my

stomach again. "Larry!" I grabbed his arm just as the figure saw us and turned and hurried into the woods.

"What's the matter?" Larry looked at me. "What's the matter with you, Kip?"

"I just saw the fog man," I said. "He just went into the woods up there!"

"So what?" Larry pulled his arm away. "I told you he's always prowling somewhere at dawn."

"But, Larry," I said, hardly able to believe the words I was about to say, "it was the fog man all right, but he wasn't bent over! He wasn't even limping!"

CHAPTER SIX

"You must be kidding!" Larry took the blanket off his head and looked up the road.

"No!" My voice rose. "I tell you, Larry, he was walking like you or me—he wasn't bent over!"

Larry shook his head. "You must have imagined it—you only thought it was the fog man." He narrowed his eyes and stared at the empty road. "That old guy has been here more than three years—he always limps."

"But he wasn't limping just then, and I know it was the fog man. He had the same brown coat, the same ragged hat, and the same white beard." I said again, "I know it was the fog man."

Larry looked at me strangely. "I think you're tired," he said. "You had a long trip here, we got up early your first morning, and we hardly slept at all last night. You're just tired."

"I am *not* tired!" It was all I could do to keep myself from stomping my foot like a two-year-old. "I saw him, plain as day. He *ran* when he saw us."

"So what do you want to do about it?"

That question stopped me. Actually, what could we do about it? If the old man pretended that he was crippled, what business did we have interfering? I shrugged my shoulders. "Guess there's nothing we can do," I said. "We've got enough to do just worrying about this robbery." I walked on, then stopped again as Larry reached my side. "But isn't it queer?" I asked myself as well as my cousin. "Why would he want to do a thing like that?"

Larry walked on. "I still say you're just tired."

"You don't believe me then?"

"Oh, I think you really *thought* you saw him," Larry told me, "but I don't know whether you really did see him or not."

I felt my neck flush; I walked past him silently. We walked single file for several blocks. Then Larry strode up beside me.

"Let's not act this way," he said. "My gosh, I'm so glad you came to visit—I'd hate to have it all spoiled because of something silly like this. I'm sorry, Kip. I guess you really did see him."

I felt the stiffness go out of my body; anger always makes me feel hard all over. "It's okay," I said. "I guess it did sound kind of crazy. But you really were right about one thing—I am pretty tired."

"Me too! Sitting up all night nearly killed me. We'll have to eat something hot—then maybe we'll feel like going back to the hut again. Karminsky will have to go there sooner or later." He paused, then added, "I just hope it isn't later. Sure would be good if all this ended while you were still here."

"We still have time," I said. "Something is sure to happen soon."

We walked on, our paces matched, silent again.

47

But this silence was a friendly one, and there can be a world of difference in that!

When we walked into the house we found Uncle Matt in the kitchen having coffee. He peered over his paper at us. "You look a little wet." He laughed. "When the rain woke me, the first thing I thought about was that camp area. Looks like you really got soaked."

"Yeah, we're wet all right!" Larry took my blanket

and started down the cellar steps. "I'll hang our beds up to dry," he called back.

Uncle Matt put down his paper. "You had enough of this rough life? I'm just about worn out myself—Ludington's had more excitement in the last two days than it usually has in a year."

"It hasn't been bad," I said, thinking at the same time how bad it really had been. I tried to find the things for breakfast, but I was more interested in

the latest news than I was in eating right then. "Find anything in the cars leaving town?" I asked.

Uncle Matt frowned, then rubbed his eye. "Not a thing." He stopped, then smiled. "And I've looked in more trunks than an elephant nose doctor." I had to smile, although not because of the quip: it just seemed funny that he could think I'd be fooled by his jokes. Anybody could see how worried he was.

"What are the plans for today?" Larry came upstairs and began getting things for breakfast.

"We'll search the woods," Uncle Matt said. "We think Karminsky must be hiding out nearby—he didn't have a car, so he must have walked. If someone else helped him out, then there'll be tire tracks back in the woods. Any way we look at it, we figure he's still in the area. And the money must be here too."

"There's a lot of woods to search, Dad. You could never look everywhere."

"We figured that out too. Karminsky has to have water—he might have hidden water as well as food, but we doubt it. We figure that he's camping out near a water supply. Also we figure that he's fairly close to a road. When he thinks the roads are clear, he'll want to get away quick."

Larry looked at me. I tried to continue eating without looking up. The hut we found had everything that they were looking for.

Uncle Matt stood. "You boys better lie down for a while. You both look as if you could use some sleep. There's a casserole in the refrigerator for your lunch. I may not be back until late." He stopped at the door, then shook his head, almost looking disappointed. "Guess I had you two mapped out wrong," he said. "I thought sure you'd ask to come along."

I shifted uncomfortably. "We're too beat!" Larry said, laughing. "Good luck, though, Pop. We'll be waiting to hear what happens."

As soon as the door shut, I turned to Larry. "Think they'll find the hut?"

He reached for more toast, then answered. "I think they'll feel just like I did. Remember how I said it was foolish to check such an easy place? I bet they won't look inside either. Besides, there's so many places to look, they may not even get near that old lumber camp."

"Do you think we should go back now?"

Larry paused. "I don't think so, now that we know the search is on. There'll be a lot of people out and somebody might see us going there. We'd better wait until later. The search probably won't go on after dark. Nobody could see anything then anyway."

I ate slowly, still thinking of the hut, of the crippled figure suddenly walking upright, and of possible connections between the two ideas. Finally, unable to keep my thoughts to myself any longer, I spoke. "Do you suppose the fog man has anything to do with all this?" I asked.

Larry laughed, almost spilling his milk. "That old guy? Not on your life! He has all he can do to carry his driftwood!"

I smiled, but said nothing. I wasn't quite so sure he was as harmless as everybody seemed to think.

"I do think it would be a good idea to lie down, though," Larry said, suddenly serious. If we want to go out to the hut tonight, we'll have to get some sleep now."

"I'm not really sleepy," I said, because I felt more tired than sleepy; but I went to Larry's room and the two of us lay down on the twin beds. In minutes Larry was asleep. I lay quietly for nearly an hour, my mind revolving like a kaleidoscope with hiccoughs, then I dropped off myself.

Hours later, I felt someone shaking me. "Kip! Kipper!" I opened my eyes and found Larry bending over me. The lights were on—it was early evening.

"I'm awake," I said, for Larry continued to shake me. His eyes were wide and excited.

"Dad's home," he reported. "We've slept all day! I just went to ask him about the search. They didn't find Karminsky!"

"Well, you didn't think they would," I said, sitting up.

"Yes, but get this! I hinted about that old lumber camp—asked Dad if anyone had searched around there today. Dad said he had done it himself. He even looked inside the hut!"

"And found?" I asked, hardly able to wait for the answer.

"Nothing!" Larry said excitedly. "He looked right inside the hut. There wasn't *anything* in there!"

CHAPTER SEVEN

"But there *must* have been!" I moved to the edge of the bed. "We were just there this morning and that hut was loaded with food."

"It's gone now!"

"The fog man!" I said. "Do you suppose that he——"

Larry shook his head. "He doesn't have anything to do with this, Kipper. I tell you that Karminsky was out there all the time! I'm sure of it!" Larry's eyes were wide, his face flushed. "He didn't go near the hut until he was sure we were gone. Somehow he knew that we were there, so he hid out nearby. When

53

he saw us leave, he hurried back to the hut and moved everything out."

I thought back to the waiting. *Had there been any noises to give us away?* "We were awfully quiet during those few hours," I said.

"Oh, what's the difference how he knew we were there? The point is, we really had found his hideout after all—and we very nearly found him too. We should have stayed there even in the rain."

"Did you tell your dad?"

"No! My gosh, Kip, I'm trying to do this on my own. Dad doesn't have the least idea that we're mixed up in this case. He'd have a fit if he knew. I want to do all this without his help, and I think we can. I've got an idea how we can solve the whole case."

I tied my shoes and looked up. "Okay, what's the plan?" I hoped I sounded more agreeable than I felt. For some reason, Larry's reasoning didn't seem quite right to me, but I didn't want to let him know—at the time I didn't have any better ideas to offer anyway.

Larry was too happy to notice my lack of enthusiasm. People who are very happy always think everyone around them shares the same state. "We'll leave as soon as Dad goes to bed," he said. "He knows we slept all day, so he expects we'll want to do something tonight. Let him think we're going to the second show at the movies. Then we'll get some flashlights and go back out to the hut. Karminsky had a lot of stuff to carry, so he couldn't have gone far from

54

it—he must still be pretty close to the hut. If we can find out where he's hiding, then we'll practically have the whole case solved for Dad."

"I don't know, Larry," I said hesitantly. "Do you really think we'll find anything out there now?"

Larry started toward the door. "Only one way to find out, isn't there?" He winked as he walked out.

We ate the casserole, but I'm not sure whether it was our breakfast, lunch, or dinner.

It was after nine o'clock that night when we left the house. We never actually lied to Uncle Matt, but somehow we led him to believe that we were going to the movies. Truth is something that stands still—if you move fast enough you can go completely around it, yet look as though you have been standing right on it all the time. We went toward the lake, making plans to stay on the main road until we reached the spot that we knew would lead right to the hut.

It was a strange night. The moon was full, making a light almost as bright as the sun, but at the lake a heavy fog was rising off the water, covering all of the shoreline and half of the beach area. The foghorn was blowing mournfully and the lighthouse light flashed off and on, making the lighthouse look like a one-eyed monster standing at the end of the breakwall.

We turned at the drive along the parking area and began walking up the road. Ahead, the road was dark —near the sidewalk leading to the breakwall, the streetlights gave off a small glow, which barely cut through the fog. As far up the parking lot as I could see, rows of silent dark cars were parked. "How come all the cars are here now?" I asked.

Larry laughed. "Those are the older kids," he said. "They come here at night to watch submarine races."

"What?"

"It's a big joke around here, Kip. When a fellow wants to be alone with a girl, he takes her down there by the lake and they sit watching for submarines."

"Quite a line," I said. "I'll have to remember that one for future use."

After we passed the parking area, the night seemed cooler. Sometimes just having light around makes it seem warmer, I guess. I know that as soon as we left the light, I felt a chill begin. It grew stronger and stronger as we walked farther along the dark road. Far off in the woods I could hear strange noises, but I tried to persuade myself that they were only birds. I can well understand why primitive men believed that evil lurked in the nighttime—reason seems to diminish in the darkness. We had flashlights, but we had decided not to use them unless we had to. A few cars passed us, but no one stopped.

"That guy must be pretty sure he's safe now," Larry finally said. His voice sounded husky in the darkness.

"Why?"

"He saw us leave—then probably saw the searchers there, and then saw them leave too. He must think we've given up on that area."

I slowed my pace, swallowed loudly. "Larry, I may as well tell you—I don't think you're right."

"Right? Right about what?"

I paused, trying to put my words in order before I spoke. They seemed vague even to me, but I wanted to make Larry understand. "I've been trying to figure out what happened this morning. I don't think Karminsky moved that food."

"Then who did?"

Now was the hard part. I swallowed loudly again and spoke fast, thinking that the quicker something was over, the less unpleasant it would be. "I've been trying to tell you, Larry. There's something fishy about that old guy who's been prowling around here. I *know* he doesn't really limp. I guess I might be silly, but I think that somehow he's in on this robbery. Remember—I saw him at the beach just before the boat docked yesterday too."

Larry walked a few seconds without speaking. "I'm trying to see it the way you do," he finally said. "To me he's just a funny old man. He seems to be something altogether different to you."

"Well, he *is* something different, Larry! No normal old man would pretend to be a cripple!"

"But why would he limp around here for three years pretending to be something he isn't?"

"And why would he move Karminsky's food?"

"It must have been Karminsky's food," Larry mumbled as we walked along. "It couldn't have been anybody else's. The fog man buys food all the time, but he's never had enough money to buy that much at once. He just lives from day to day . . . he buys a few cans every other week or so. Nobody else would leave that stuff way out here."

We were so involved in asking each other questions that we almost passed our entrance to the woods. We had to backtrack a few steps and we entered through the same hedge we had found early that morning.

A forest at night is different—different from a forest in the daylight, different from the forest most people picture in memory. It isn't gay or airy or free at night. The blackness seems to change the forms and color of everything. Even the smells are odd—there's a musky odor, a damp feeling, a creepy sensation. Innocent things appear as medieval monsters and dangerous animals seem to lurk in every crevice.

"Spooky, huh?" Larry reached for my flashlight. "Let's just use yours now," he whispered. "Mine's brighter and I'd rather wait awhile before we turn it on."

We crept along like two black shadows, pointing the flashlight at the ground, covering the end with our hands, making our fingers shine in bloody splendor. The moon was bright above the trees but, except for a few clearings, the forest was pitch black.

It was almost impossible to see anything except the direct circle of light emphasized at our feet. The ground seemed covered with footprints, but when we turned toward the lumber camp, we saw most of the prints disappear in other directions. At last we saw the hut ahead, yawning and deserted-looking.

Cautiously, with the flashlight off, using the moonlight for guidance, we crept forward to the hut.

"Now!" Larry spoke and flashed the light simultaneously. The beam leaped into the darkness of the hideout.

"Nothing!" Larry's voice sounded surprised, as though, even yet, he had expected to find something inside.

We stared at the emptiness, then Larry sighed. "This was as far as Dad went," he said. "He didn't know this was the place to search thoroughly, so I think he just looked around casually. Let's each go different ways now and meet back here. Look for footprints, a new trail, or any of that canned stuff. Karminsky's got to be around here somewhere."

Larry handed me his more powerful light and turned to the right. I followed, turned left, and stepped into the darkness alone.

My skin crawled. It really did—I felt goose bumps rise and fall like the skin of a crawling snake. I was cold, but my hands were sweaty. I beamed the light to the ground and began searching.

The rain had not evaporated in the deeper parts of the woods. Puddles stood everywhere and the sand was wet and soggy. I tried to forget my fears, but I kept remembering Larry's stories about quicksand. I walked carefully, cautiously, like a baby walking on ice.

In relief I saw that I was near the back of the hut. I could barely make out the flicker of a light, but I knew that Larry was coming closer. Knowing he was near gave me courage. I began walking farther back into the denser part of the woods, flashing my light ahead of me to the right and the left.

Only the corner of my eye saw something, but instinctively I rushed the light back to a dark clump that did not seem to belong to the trees. What was it? I stood motionless, staring at the bundle lying huddled on the forest floor. Was it—could it possibly be a man? Karminsky?

Cautiously I stepped forward. Was the clump moving? No. My heart was pounding and I heard my own breathing. My light beam quivered in my shaking hand.

As I moved nearer I realized it was not a man. The last steps I ran. Unbelievingly, I threw my flashlight down and grabbed the objects. "Larry!" I shouted wildly. "Larry!"

"What happened?" I saw his light, heard him crashing through the forest, but my senses were too numb to answer. I sat clutching half of the objects, still too shocked to realize what they really meant.

I heard Larry gasp beside me. "No!" he said, his voice a hoarse whisper. "It can't be!"

But it was. I held a long brown coat, a brown hat, and brown pants. And lying on the ground, looking even whiter against the black of the forest floor, was the long white beard of the fog man.

CHAPTER EIGHT

It is this second—this scene—that haunts me now: the dark, damp night, the glimmering flashlights, the moving shadows, Larry crashing through the underbrush, and that beard, that white, innocent-looking beard, lying motionless at my feet. It almost seemed as though I was staring at a dead body, as though the old man himself lay sprawled there on the ground.

Larry grabbed the beard. "False!" he exclaimed, his voice echoing in the stillness. "A false beard!"

I held out the clothes. "It's everything he wore," I said.

"But why?" Larry began flashing his light over the ground, as if the forest itself could answer his question. But we saw nothing. The rain had turned the ground to mud, and if there had been footprints they were no longer there.

"Then you were right," Larry murmured. "Something really was fishy around here this morning."

I nodded, too puzzled to answer.

"I've been wrong all along," Larry said quietly. "All along."

"But how could you have known the truth?" I said, finally finding my voice. "You didn't know what was going on."

"And I wouldn't listen to you this morning when you tried to tell me." Larry stuffed the beard in his jacket and stared at the ground.

"The searchers didn't find this stuff this morning," I said. "They missed things, too. You're not the only one who's made a mistake."

Larry shook his head. "That poor old guy," he said in a whisper. "That poor harmless old guy."

I felt my stomach tighten. "Harmless?" I said. "Can't you see what this find really means? He wasn't a poor harmless old man at all. I told you he doesn't even limp! He was pretending all this time."

Larry gave me a strange look. "You mean you still think that the fog man was involved in that robbery?"

"Well, sure I do. Can't you see that? This disguise proves that he was involved. He got rid of it, didn't he?"

Larry took the clothes from my hands. "How do you know who got rid of it?"

"Well, who else would wear this outfit?"

Larry stared at me, his face pale in the flickering beam of his flashlight. "I'll tell you who," he said. "Karminsky."

I caught my breath. "Karminsky!"

"Think back to the day of the robbery," Larry said.

"I am thinking back to yesterday morning," I answered. "That's why I know the fog man was involved. I *saw* him walking toward the dock before we went up for bait. I *know* he must have been near those shipyards."

"So was Karminsky," Larry answered quickly. "And now what do we have? We have Karminsky missing and a set of clothes that belonged to the fog man. We have a false beard. Can't you see it? Karminsky disguised himself. He knew all along about the old guy who prowled around our beaches. What would stop him from buying a false beard and having it ready when he left the boat docks? He could hang around the woods until he spotted the old guy, get rid of him, and parade all over Ludington in his outfit. Anybody could look like the fog man in that getup. Karminsky wouldn't have to worry about hiding out at all. It would look like he had completely disappeared from this area."

"Then why throw the clothes away?" I asked, trying to follow Larry's logic.

"Because you saw him this morning when he wasn't limping. He knew that we'd be on the lookout for the fog man now."

I started to ask something else, then stopped. A question had just flooded my brain, but I wasn't sure that I wanted to hear the answer.

Larry was strangely silent too, so I hesitantly asked, "And the real fog man then? What happened to him?"

"I don't know, Kip. I just don't know." Larry had lost the excitement in his voice. He shook his head and leaned against a tree.

"Maybe we can figure out a lot of the answers if we start right back at the beginning," I said. "We were right near the docks when everything happened. Maybe we saw something and didn't realize then how important it would be."

I stopped, trying to transport myself back to yesterday—to the foggy, eerie morning when I had first seen the brown, lumbering figure. "The fog man was heading toward the shipyards when the robbery was taking place," I said slowly, speaking aloud the thoughts I was only just then forming. "Karminsky was leaving the yards at the same time that the fog man was heading toward them. But that's as far as I can think it through. What happened then?"

Larry sighed. "We can't really know, I guess, but it seems certain that they must have met." He pulled a leaf from a branch and began shredding it. "There are bushes all along that beach path though," he said, pausing after each word. "Those bushes might mean something."

"Bushes!" I said, almost disgusted with Larry. "I'm

talking about a meeting between these two men and you're talking about the scenery."

"Maybe those bushes mean something," Larry said without looking up from his hands. His voice thickened. "Maybe Karminsky became the fog man right there beside the beach path."

"But we were there!" I said. "We ran right up that path!"

"Sure, and so did everybody else!" Larry threw down the leaf skeleton and pulled another branch down. "Everybody ran toward the docks, remember? And remember how you admitted later that you hadn't even seen the very things that you vaulted over on your way to the docks? Remember that boat wreck that you never even saw? That's how it was with all of us. We were so interested in that boat whistle that maybe we missed the most important thing of all."

"But there was a fellow in a rowboat, Larry, that guy from the boat. He was right out off the shoreline —he would have seen something."

"But he ran in, too. Remember? He even fell overboard, he was so anxious to get to shore. And it was still foggy when all of this was going on. I think Karminsky had the fog man right beside that path and everybody was so interested in running to the docks that nobody even saw them."

I swallowed loudly. "You think that while we were in that bait house, before we ran up the path, Karminsky met and k-killed that old guy?"

Larry sighed. "Oh, how should I know! I'm only guessing, Kipper. But it all fits in, doesn't it? That's what we're trying to do now, right? We're just guessing at what really happened. They must have met, because we know they both must have been there at the same time. We know that Karminsky hasn't been found and we know that the fog man has suddenly stopped limping—it seems that there is only one answer to all of that."

I nodded, then watched Larry pull the beard from his jacket and throw it on the ground.

"Let's get out of here," I finally said. Again in my mind I saw the lonely, faltering figure. Had he seemed strange and unreal because death was so near? Had I sensed something waiting for him? I shook my head and started to walk away. It seemed foolish to stand there any longer. If Karminsky had been there earlier—which it seemed he had, for the beard was evidence of that—he had long since left. Larry followed me from the clearing.

We moved noiselessly through the shrubbery, pausing only long enough to find our way. All through the dark trek, my mind was racing, but it kept returning to one idea. Unspoken thoughts don't seem as frightening as spoken ones, but they seem to cause a lot more worry when left unsaid. Finally I had to ask. "Well, what happened to the real fog man then?"

Larry paused, looked back. "What about him?" he said.

I looked at the ground. "His body," I whispered, unconsciously feeling the need to only whisper the words. "Where is it?"

Larry sighed and looked away. "You mean you haven't been able to guess?"

"No," I said loudly. "There can't be a body in the bushes now; somebody would have found it. Karminsky couldn't have dragged it very far; somebody would have seen him."

"The lake," Larry said simply. He began moving again. "Nobody was on the breakwater. After we all ran to the docks, he simply dragged him out on the wall, weighted him down, and tossed him in. There's plenty of cement blocks around."

I moved on, saying nothing, thinking everything, feeling strangely hollow and sad inside.

It was almost midnight when we reached the parking area around the lake. The lighthouse was still blinking, the foghorn was still blowing, but somehow the scene looked different. It wasn't innocent any longer. Somewhere out off the breakwall . . . but I didn't let myself think anymore. I silently followed Larry through the quiet streets.

"I think we should tell Dad that Karminsky was disguised as the fog man," Larry said at last. "Maybe he'll want to drag the lake near the breakwall."

I nodded, scraping my shoes as we moved along, dreading our talk with Uncle Matt. "I wish we had more to tell," I said. "He'll be sleeping and it means that we'll have to wake him up. The story sounds funny now that we're out of that woods. In the woods it seemed a lot more real."

"He's going to wonder why we didn't bring that stuff, I bet," Larry answered. "I don't know why I threw it away—it seemed creepy, I guess."

I nodded, knowing exactly what he meant but realizing the words were impossible to say.

We turned the corner to Larry's street. "Look!" Larry shouted, grabbing my arm. "The lights are on at the house. Dad must be up—something's going on!"

We began running up the street. We reached the house and jumped the steps to the porch. Larry flung open the front door.

Uncle Matt was at the desk, his hand on the telephone, his pajamas wrinkled, his eyes sleepy.

"What happened? What did you hear?"

Uncle Matt began rubbing his eye. "They've found Karminsky," he answered. "Kewaunee just called headquarters. They arrested him in a bar over there an hour ago."

"Kewaunee?" Larry's face grew pale.

"That's right. Karminsky claims that he never left there, and he has a pretty good alibi. The Kewaunee police say they can hold him a few hours for questioning, so I'd like to get over there myself. I want to get to the bottom of this case. If he really did miss the boat yesterday, when the car ferry was robbed, then we're going to have to start all over again."

"Can you get over there to question him, Dad?"

"I called the ticket office at the boat dock here. I can get the midnight boat over in twenty minutes and be back early tomorrow afternoon, but I don't know whether I should leave you two alone here the rest of the night. It's too late to get anybody to come in."

I was too shocked to answer. How could Karminsky be disguised as the fog man one morning and be in Kewaunee that evening? How could he get there?

"How did he get to Kewaunee?" Larry asked before I could speak.

"That's the part I want to find out," Uncle Matt said, rubbing his eye. "It seems like he must be telling the truth—he missed the boat and was left there."

"Go ahead and go, Dad," Larry said. "I'd like to get the whole story myself."

"We'll talk it out in the bedroom," Uncle Matt answered, getting up from the chair. "Come on in."

Larry turned to follow his father. "If Karminsky missed the boat, I think we must have missed it somewhere, too," he whispered as he passed me.

CHAPTER NINE

I sat alone in the living room while Larry and his father talked in the bedroom. I could hear Uncle Matt opening drawers and getting dressed, but his voice was muffled and meaningless, and I understood nothing he said. The thoughts that were reeling in my brain were every bit as meaningless as the mumbles from the bedroom. Senseless facts kept darting in and out of my consciousness—*Karminsky is not the fog man . . . Karminsky is in Kewaunee . . . he could not be the thief . . . who then is the thief? . . . and who had disguised himself as the fog man? . . . and why?* I shifted uncomfortably on the couch. When I can't solve a mental problem, I can't be content physically either.

"I hate to run off like this, Christopher," Uncle Matt said, coming back into the living room, "but Larry has persuaded me that you can get along until tomorrow. I should be back shortly after noon. Larry has the telephone number of the office—somebody is always there if you need help."

I nodded, trying to reassure him. He was dressed in his uniform now and he seemed to be a different man. It's strange how quickly clothes can seem to change a man's personality.

Uncle Matt turned, put his arm across Larry's shoulders, and hesitated, as though he wanted to say something more. He frowned, then walked to the closet. "There's plenty of food here," he said, and I knew he hadn't said what he wanted to say. He took his hat and walked toward the front door. "I'm sure I can trust you boys," he said softly. Then he waved his hand and shut the door.

"Can you beat that!" Larry stopped acting the part of the innocent bystander and became the guilty conspirator again. He flopped on the couch beside me and sighed. "We work this whole deal out and find that our main suspect might have been all the way across the lake when the robbery took place."

He sounded so disappointed that Karminsky might be innocent that I had to laugh. "We don't know for sure," I said. "Let's wait until your dad gets back before we give up the ship."

For a few minutes we sat without speaking, both of us puzzled. Why would anyone be disguised as the fog man unless he was somehow connected with the robbery? The way that we had worked out the day of the theft must have been the way things had really happened. Somebody had to run from the docks carrying the stolen money, since the bag wasn't found in the shipyard search; somebody had to meet the fog man on that path, since I had seen him on the beach that morning heading toward the docks; somebody had certainly bought a false beard, since we had already found it.

At last Larry cleared his throat and spoke. "I've

71

thought it all out, Kip, and I still think that the fog man was dumped off that breakwall right after the robbery. He must have seen something going on down there. I don't know where the false beard fits in this picture, but I do think that the bottom of the lake near the breakwall should be searched."

I nodded, certain now that Larry was right. "You should have told your dad," I said. "We'll never know what's down there until it's all searched. The police force could do it in an hour."

"It's going to be searched down there all right, Kip." Larry stood, walked to the window. "I've got an idea." Excitement made his voice crack.

"What?"

"I'm going to search under the water there myself."

"*Larry*!" I shouted his name and the word sounded even louder in the small room. "You can't go searching underwater all by yourself—you'll never find anything alone. Let your dad and his men do it."

"But what if we're wrong, Kip? What if we've got the whole plot figured out wrong and Dad and his force go down there and search for nothing but a figment of our imagination? The whole city would laugh at a bunch of cops skin diving off the wall after nothing but a dream. But if I do it, who's to know? Who's to care? It won't matter if I find anything or not. We can't be positive until we actually find the fog man, so we have to go look ourselves."

"But they won't let you dive off the breakwall out there by the fishing area. Somebody is sure to stop you."

"That's just it, Cousin, nobody is going to see me." Larry pulled down the window shade and started toward the bedroom. "I'm not going to do this searching when anyone is around to stop me. I'm doing it tonight."

"Tonight! But you can't go down there tonight. It's after midnight!"

"What of it? I'll start out near the lighthouse end, dive in, and follow the wall to the bottom. If there's anything there, it will be near the wall and I'll be sure to feel it on my way down. I don't need daylight."

I swallowed hard. "You can't do it, Larry. Uncle Matt wouldn't like it."

"Dad won't even have to know about it if we don't find anything. If we do find the body, then he'll be too busy to worry about it. Besides, he didn't specifically say that I shouldn't dive off the breakwall tonight."

I made a face. "You sure can twist things around to suit yourself," I said almost admiringly. "But it really is dangerous, Larry. You can't joke about that."

"We'll take our flashlights and you can guide me along until I've reached the end of the wall on both sides. Nobody would dump a body near the swimming area, so we only have to search from the lighthouse to the diving board. That won't take so long. Nobody will even have to know that we're going."

I watched Larry fling off his clothes and reach for his bathing trunks. I started to speak twice, then changed my mind. The time for persuading him to stop was past. In fact, I realized then that the time for persuading him to stop had never started. The minute the plan had formed in his mind was the minute his decision to search by himself had been made. Larry was obsessed with the idea of helping Uncle Matt find the stolen money and nothing I or anybody else could say or do was going to stop him.

"Well, how about it?" Larry turned from his closet, pulling his clothes over his bathing trunks. "You going to take care of the light for me?"

"Sure," I said. "Just lead the way."

We walked back up the same street, silent now and dark. There wasn't a light in any of the houses and no cars were running on the streets. It seemed as though the city had quietly closed its doors and moved on.

You can smell Lake Michigan blocks away. It's a clean smell, the kind that makes you want to draw in lungfuls of air and let it out very slowly. The temperature gets cooler the nearer you get to the lake and the wind seems heavier and damper. Straight ahead I saw the water. The moonlight only caught the surface of a few large waves, but the whole lake seemed alive and moving. There was no fog. The lighthouse was sending out a steady stream of light, blinking off, blinking on. Far off in the water we could see the rear lights of the car ferry that Uncle Matt had taken to Kewaunee.

We left the main street, walked on the sandy beach,

and stepped up on the breakwall. We had not spoken. There was no one around. Up on the hill we could see the empty parking lot. We might have been explorers discovering a new sea in a land without men.

Our shoes echoed against the cement as we walked out on the wall. The waves lapped against the sides, making queer gurgling sounds, like an animal before a meal. My hands began to sweat. I slowed my pace.

"Here we are." Larry whispered, even though there was no one to hear but me. It seemed—it almost seemed—as though the lake itself might be listening.

Larry began removing his clothes. He tossed them in the doorway of the lighthouse, for the door was shut and barred. And then he stood in just his trunks, his pale body reflecting the light from the beacon. "You just stand as near the edge as you can and hold the light near the water." Larry was still whispering. "I'll slip off the side and follow the wall down to the bottom."

"Larry," I asked hesitantly, "are you really sure you want to go through with this?"

His eyes gleamed in the moonlight. For a second they seemed the same as the gleaming water in the lake; then he blinked. "I have to do it," he said. "I'll be all right. I've been diving and holding my breath since I was a kid."

Like a shadow, he crept down the wall to the fishing ledge. I followed, turning on the flashlight. The light beacon blinked on and off over our heads. The foghorn was silent.

"Just hold it steady," Larry said. "When I come up, we'll move down the wall a few feet." Then he was gone.

It was unbelievable how easily he slipped into the restless waters. One second he was there, the next second he was gone, and hardly a ripple showed where he had disappeared. It was as though he had never been. I hung over the edge, hardly daring to breathe.

"Ye-owie! It's cold!" Larry popped up, amost hitting his head on the flashlight. He shook his hair from his eyes. "Move on, Kip," he called and disappeared again.

I don't know how many times he came up, then went down again. I don't think I was sane enough to count. All I cared about was seeing his head pop up suddenly through the black waters. Twice again I tried to persuade him to stop. The longer I crouched on the wall, the more sinister the lake seemed to become. I began thinking about the silent whirlpool that could be deep under the water. I faced the lake as though it were an enemy. It seemed to be waiting . . . waiting for what?

We were getting near the diving board—half of our job was done. Two more dives, then we could start on the other side of the wall and finish up. I was beginning to breathe normally again. Even fear, if faced constantly, loses some of its edge.

"One more time," Larry said near the swimming area. He took a deep breath and disappeared beneath the water. In the light I saw the white of his body go down, then everything was black. I hung over the edge with the light, waiting for him to come bobbing to the surface. All around me the lake was making sucking noises, the water seemed alive and hungry.

I don't know how long I kneeled peering into the empty water. I don't know what finally convinced me that Larry was not coming up. Suddenly, I knew he could not still be alive after being underwater that long without air; suddenly I tasted the blood I had forced from my lip; suddenly I knew my sore knees could mean only one thing—I had stared so long into the black nothingness that enough time had passed to prove that Larry was never coming up again.

Should I have jumped in after him? Would it really have mattered? I don't know if I thought of diving into the water myself. I don't know what I thought. I only recall sitting back on my heels, swallowing the blood from my lip, and feeling tears helplessly begin to roll down my face.

CHAPTER TEN

"Kipper!"

I stopped breathing. The world stood still.

"It's me, Kip."

I stood, my knees trembling, and frantically began to wave the light over the waves. *Could it be that Larry was still miraculously alive? But no . . . there was nothing . . . no one.* My throat tightened. I clenched my teeth. But who had spoken? The voice had sounded distant and like an echo, but it had been a voice. The hairs on the back of my neck stood up, and I shook my head to clear my thoughts. I flopped on my stomach again and peered deep into the water. Nothing . . . no one. Was I going insane?

"Can you hear me?"

It *was* Larry! I was sure now that he was calling me; but how could he still be alive? And where was he? "Where are you?" I shouted to the empty air, my voice cracking.

"You won't believe it, Kipper, you just won't believe it!"

Larry's voice was filled with excitement. I stared up the wall. Had he surfaced farther down? But no . . . nothing . . . no one.

"Larry!" I shouted. "I can't see you!"

"I'm in the wall. Inside the breakwall!"

The flashlight fell from my hands and dropped into the water. The splash it made was the only sound. I stared at the solid cement beneath my feet. "In the wall? You're inside this wall?"

"And so is something else!" The voice floated eerily up from the cement. "Hang on, Kip, I'm coming up."

I stood for a second, too confused to know what to think. Then I ran back to the ledge, knelt down, and peered back into the black water.

"We've done it!" Larry suddenly popped to the surface, his teeth gleaming in a ghostly smile. "Take a look!" He pulled himself up onto the ledge, and threw down a large bag between us. Without another word, he ripped open the plastic protection and held the bag in front of me. The lighthouse light flashed on, illuminating the inside of the bag momentarily.

"Money!" I shouted. "It's the money!"

Larry laughed out loud. "We went fishing for a minnow and we caught a whale!" I was so glad that he was all right—I had been so scared just moments before—that Larry's remark seemed hilarious to me and I laughed so hard I nearly fell off the ledge.

"But how did you do it?" I finally managed to ask. "How could you breathe? How did you get inside the wall? Is it all hollow under there?" Once started on my questions, I couldn't stop long enough even to let him answer.

"It was really an accident, Kip." Larry closed the bag and held it tightly against his chest. "When I was feeling the side of the wall under the water, I felt this big opening. I decided to swim inside to see how big it was in there. When I got past the cement wall, I realized that it was all hollow in that spot—sort of like a shell. I swam to the top of the water and found myself inside the breakwater—the top of it was above my head. There's about three feet of space in there between the wall and the water."

"Three feet! My gosh, Larry, you took a chance doing that! What if there hadn't been any air inside there?"

"Well, I was pretty glad there was air, believe me. I was just starting to take a deep breath so I could swim out of there, when I felt something bobbing against my shoulder. It was a bag tied to the underwater supports. I knew right away what it must be."

"The money," I said.

Larry smiled despite his chattering teeth. "Yeah, the money. Isn't it great? I can't wait to show Dad . . . he'll go crazy. We'd better get this money out of here now. Do you think we can wait till Dad comes tomorrow? Oh, Kip, I just can't wait to see his face. I wonder who put it there."

We ran over to Larry's clothes while Larry kept on talking. "Dad will never believe it!" He began dressing, moving about in a queer half-dance, for he still held the bag and he passed it from one hand to the other while he pulled on his clothes.

I watched him in silence, feeling awed that he treated the money so casually. Finally I spoke. "Where will we take the bag at this hour, Larry?"

"Home."

"To your house? Gosh, Larry, that doesn't sound good to me. I think we should take it somewhere. That's an awful lot of money."

"We *are* taking it somewhere," he said. "It's going home with us. Dad's safe is better than a bank." He folded both arms around the bag. "I'll take care of it all right."

"I don't like being responsible for that much money," I said, louder. "I think we should tell someone at your father's office."

Larry came closer to me. In the light from the beacon, still flashing on and off, I saw his face, pale and determined. "Don't tell anyone about this, Kipper," he said slowly. "I told you I want to take care of this case myself."

"But you can't do anything else," I said. "You have the money—that's enough.

"No, it isn't." Larry turned and began walking along the breakwall. "I want to find the thief, too. I've got to figure out a way to get him."

You'll never do it, I wanted to say. *You can't possibly do it*. But I said nothing. I followed Larry silently, for by then I knew that Larry had never learned the meaning of the word *can't*.

CHAPTER ELEVEN

Larry hardly spoke on the way home. He walked quickly, almost running through the dark streets, clutching the bag tightly. "I'm going to think of a way to trap that guy," he said once, but I could think of nothing to answer. I walked behind him feeling like a shadow, full of dark opinions but powerless to speak.

He was smiling when we reached his house. "We made it without anyone seeing us," he said softly as we went up the steps. He pointed to the nearby dark houses. "You worried for nothing. They've slept through everything we've done. *Now* are you glad we went?"

I had to smile in answer. That Larry! I'm smiling now when I think of how he looked that night on the porch—his hair, still wet, hanging on his forehead; his clothes wrinkled; his arms wrapped around that plastic bag; and his face stretched into one huge, gleaming grin. It was impossible to be worried when he was around.

Later, in the kitchen, we made hot chocolate. The money was locked in Uncle Matt's safe and we were both dry again. Neither of us was sleepy though; I felt like a toy that had been wound up too tight—everything inside of me was taut.

"Wish I could figure out how we could trap this thief," Larry said, more to himself than to me. Clad in a blue bathrobe, he sat stirring his chocolate, staring off into space.

"I keep thinking about the fog man," I said. "Do you think that old guy is really dead?"

Larry stirred faster. "I don't know, Kip. Every time I try to think things through, I get all confused. I wish we could just try to figure out what happened without even thinking about him. He just gets in the way when I try to figure out that robbery."

I sat back, trying to imagine the robbery without first seeing the eerie figure stumbling through the fog, but I found that I could not. I could still see him in my mind's eye—first the bent, crippled old man, then the upright, straight figure near the woods. *What part did he play? Did he fit in the picture? Why did he bother me so?*

Larry wasn't waiting for my ideas. "As I see it," he was saying, "a worker on the *Wolverine* took that bag and passed it to someone on shore. Then he hightailed it over to the wall, dove in, tied it up, and went on his merry way. Maybe he saw the fog man—I don't know, but since no workers seem to be missing, that's the only way that bag could have left the shipyards.

"But no one will ever be able to prove who did it,"

I observed. "Any one of the workers could have passed that bag to someone on shore. Now that we've found the money, the thieves will never even go near that wall again."

Larry smiled. "But nobody else knows we have the money, Kipper. Nobody but you and me."

"A lot of good that does," I said. "We can't get

the thief or his buddy to go back to check whether the bag is there—that would be a sure sign of guilt."

Larry nodded, then narrowed his eyes and began speaking slowly, softly, as though his words were clay and he was trying to build a monument. "Maybe we can get one of them to check that wall, after all. We know where the money was hidden because

we found it—the thief knows where the money is because he hid it there. Now what would make him hurry to the hiding place to get it out of there right away?"

"He'd come if he thought it was in danger of being found," I answered. "He'd come if he thought it might be discovered by accident."

"Right!" Larry's eyes shone. "And just by coming to move that bag, a man would be proving he was guilty of putting it there." Larry seemed to be making plans even as he spoke.

"Sure, he would, Larry—and that's just why nobody will ever claim that bag. If we announce a search in that area, he'll stay as far away from there as possible. He'll want the money, sure, but he'll want his freedom even more."

"But what if people are searching for something else—something that has nothing to do with the robbery?"

"What else?" I asked. "What else could we announce a search for in the breakwall?"

"Me," Larry said calmly.

And then he explained his plan to me. As I sat there wide-eyed, he told me the part that he wanted me to play in his scheme for the next day. He wanted to pretend that he had drowned—wanted me to say that he had dived off the wall and disappeared. He figured that if he met his accidental death at twilight, the complete searching would be postponed until morning.

"And then," he said excitedly, "when the thief hears that the wall will be thoroughly searched in the morning, he'll try to sneak over there during the night. And you and I can be waiting!"

"You're crazy, Larry!" I cried when he had paused to take a breath. "You can't pretend you've drowned."

"I don't know why not!" He took his cup to the sink and spoke with his back to me. "It's a sure way to find out who's guilty, and it wouldn't really hurt anyone."

"Your father," I said. "It would hurt him. You can't let him think you've drowned—and he wouldn't let you try this stunt if he knew about it."

"Other people have done it," Larry argued. "We had a kid just last summer who left his clothes on the wall and pretended to have drowned. Dad spent three days down there with boats and planes looking for his body, while the kid lived it up in Muskegon."

"That doesn't mean that you can do it, too," I said. "Just because someone else has done it doesn't make it right."

"But it's for a good reason!" Larry turned to look at me—his red hair almost seemed to shoot sparks. "It's the only way to catch the thief. Maybe we could warn Dad somehow so he would know that I was really all right."

"Then he wouldn't let you do it, Larry," I said. "I know you'll try anything to flush that fellow out, but you can't do this. It'd be going too far."

Larry put his hand on my shoulder, forcing me to

meet his gaze. "Sleep on it, will you, Kip? Maybe it won't seem so bad in the morning. I could hide out in the lighthouse at the end of the wall. The whole business would only take a few hours. Will you think about it tonight?"

And so I found myself in bed, tossing and turning, while Larry slept soundly in the other bed. If I went along with his plan, the thief might be caught, but Uncle Matt would go through agony first. All kinds of people who were innocent would be caught up in the hoax, searching for a body that never was.

As I lay there trying to decide what to do, wild pictures leaped through my mind. They were only fragments because I was too tired to connect them, and a mind only half awake can never conjure up a complete scene. First the eerie figure of the fog man came parading, revealing only the body; the head came flashing next, buried in quicksand with the white beard sticking straight up like a monument; then came a blurry object sinking in water, followed by a bag of money floating through the air; and almost as real as life came Larry, deep in water, sinking and calling to me for help. I was awake, yet I was asleep; I was lying in bed, yet I was running through the past; I was walking on the razor-sharp edge of the real and the unreal, and I struggled to keep my balance. At last, near dawn, I reached a decision and I finally fell into a deep sleep.

CHAPTER TWELVE

"No." I sat in bed watching Larry. I said the word as clearly as I could, because I wanted him to see that I really meant it. "I can't go along with your idea about drowning—it would hurt too many people."

Larry walked to the bedroom window. "It's a good day," he said. "Perfect for the beach."

"Let's go swimming then," I said carefully. "But no pretending. Okay? Let's just go swimming and try to forget everything about the robbery."

Larry grinned. "You sound scared that I'll make you change your mind, Cousin." When I flushed, he added, "But I guess you're right. It was a crackpot idea all right—even I'll admit it now. The sunshine shows too many flaws—in ideas as well as everything else." He turned from the window. "When Dad comes back, I'll give him the money bag and he can turn it over to the officials. He'll have the satisfaction of doing that anyway."

I smiled, suddenly lighthearted. Having someone else agree with you can sure make you respect your own decision a lot more. We ate breakfast, made sure the safe and the house were locked, and left for the beach.

It was a great day. The beach was already full of sunbathers and swimmers. The water sparkled blue in the sunshine, not in the least resembling the black, angry lake of the night before. "Funny how the water looks so different," I said to Larry as we spread out our blanket on the sand. "Have we changed, or has it?"

"Who cares?" Larry answered. "Let's go in swimming!"

I dropped my towel and followed. There was time. enough for serious thoughts when life was not so pleasant.

We stayed in the water for an hour. It was cool but not cold, and the sun was hot. There were only small waves. I stayed fairly close to the ladder in the break-wall, but Larry bobbed up and down farther off in the water like a dolphin with red hair.

We were worn out when we came back to our blankets. I flopped down on my stomach and ran the warm sand through my fingers. "This is the life!" I said, turning over. "Here you are—a paradise right on your doorstep."

"It's all right down here, I guess," Larry answered. "I hardly ever even think about it." He rolled over onto his stomach. "Let's just lie here until we see Dad's boat coming in. I want to meet him at the dock."

We lay quietly, letting the sun soak into our wet bodies. Portable radios played on other blankets; beach balls rolled by; far away children were shouting; a lifeguard sat on a white tower with a blue flag flying overhead; sea gulls flew in the distance. I closed my eyes.

In the bright sunlight, my closed eyelids seemed full of glaring colors. *The colors are not really there,* I told myself, squinting my lids together; and the reds and the blues disappeared. I settled deeper into the sand. *Too bad the fog man couldn't be erased from my mind just as easily,* I thought drowsily. *If he were gone from my memory, then maybe I could solve the robbery.* My thoughts drifted freely . . .

The money was stolen . . . it was found in the breakwall . . . Did someone run up the beach carrying it? . . Did he dive off the wall and hide it right away? Was there any other way he could have hidden it? As I squirmed on the blanket, letting my thoughts run wild, I felt an idea slip slowly into my mind—an idea as fleeting as a moth in a garden. *Someone could have used a rowboat—but, no. The only rowboat we knew about had been used for fish-ing. But there was no fishing gear. There was a man with wet clothes, but he had a reason—he had fallen into the water. He did fall . . . or did he?*

I sat up in a single movement. "Larry!" I whispered hoarsely.

"Is the boat coming?" Larry sat up, rubbing his eyes and peering out into the water.

"Arnold Johanson!" I said. "Wasn't that his name?"

"Whose name?"

"The fellow with the rowboat!" I said impatiently. "The one who came back to the dock dripping wet."

Larry's mouth dropped open. "You mean you th——"

"I *know*!" And suddenly I did know. Who had reported that Karminsky had been on the ship out of Kewaunee? Who had disappeared as soon as the boat had docked? Who had been underwater? Who had been on the *Wolverine* long enough to know all the ins and outs?

"My gosh!" Larry said loudly. "Arnold Johanson—of course it's him! We should have known that the minute we found the money hidden in the wall. He's the only one who could have put it there. My gosh, Kipper, we've got the whole answer now!"

I nodded happily. The whole answer . . . but then my smile faded. The fog man—where did he fit in the answer that we had found? I turned to ask Larry.

"Dad's boat is coming!" Larry shouted. "We got

this thing worked out just in time. Let's go tell him!"

I started gathering our clothes, my question forgotten.

Uncle Matt looked tired when he came down the steps to the dock where Larry and I were waiting. His uniform was wrinkled and he rubbed his eyes even as he walked.

"He's innocent all right," he told us in the car. "Karminsky has been in Kewaunee since the morning he missed the *Wolverine* . . . there isn't a doubt in the world."

Larry and I said nothing. He had warned me that he wanted to tell his father about the money himself, so I knew the less I said the better it would be. I'm not a very good actor and Uncle Matt was so tired and disappointed that I kept having to force myself from shouting out the good news.

"Looks bad for the Ludington police," he said after driving a few blocks in silence. "We've been chasing the wrong man for two days." He straightened his shoulders and tried to see me in the rearview mirror. "So what's been happening here? Did you two get in some more fishing?"

Larry smiled. "We went fishing all right, Dad, but you'll never guess what we caught." His sunburned face flushed even redder than it already was.

Uncle Matt turned, frowning. "Judging from the way you two act now, I'd say you had pretty bad luck. You're too quiet to suit me." He stopped the car in front of the house. "What'd you catch? Anything we can eat for supper?"

"You sure won't be eating this!" Larry answered, laughing. "Come on in and see."

"This had better be good," Uncle Matt said, climbing out of the car.

It *was* good. The way Larry presented the bag of money, I mean. He made Uncle Matt wait until he'd washed and changed his clothes, and then, when we were settled in the living room, Larry came in and simply handed the money to his dad. "It's all there," he said almost shyly. "We counted it."

I guess I'll never see another face show as many emotions as Uncle Matt's did in that instant: surprise, shock, happiness, disbelief—they all flashed across his features as he stared at the bag. His hands fumbled as he rushed to unfold the plastic protection.

"I found it in the breakwall," Larry was saying. "Kipper and I searched down there right after you left. See, we went there to look for——"

"*In* the breakwall?" Uncle Matt stared at Larry, then at me. "*In* the breakwall?"

I nodded. "There's a hole there under the water and——"

"And the thief put the bag inside," Larry finished for me. He began jingling some coins in his pockets. "Oh, Dad, it was great! We never dreamed what we'd find!"

Uncle Matt shook his head. "But how? And who?"

"We know who put it there!" Larry shouted. "At least we think he's the only one who could have put it down under there."

"Arnold Johanson!" Uncle Matt said the name so quickly that it sounded like one word. He stood up with the bag still in his hand. "I thought that story about an overturned rowboat sounded fishy! No sailor would have an accident like that . . . Arnold Johanson! I've had my eye on him since the beginning, but I could never figure out where he put the money. There wasn't time for him to run ashore and hide it."

"Well, Kipper really figured it out," Larry said. "See, we've been trying to help out all along, but we got off on the wrong trail."

"It was the fog man," I started to say.

"That fog man turned our brains to fog!" Larry said.

Uncle Matt had hardly heard us. He was walking up and down in front of the couch. "Arnold Johanson!" he repeated over and over again. "Captain Moore will never believe it."

"When will you arrest him?" Larry asked.

Uncle Matt stopped his pacing. "Arrest him? I don't think we can arrest him, Larry."

"But why not? We know he's the thief—we know that he tried to blame Karminsky."

"But we have no proof that he actually was the thief, Son. None at all. Any one of the workers could have passed that bag to someone on shore to hide in the wall. We don't know how long it was even hidden—we can't prove anything at all."

"And that's just why we should have used my plan!" Larry said, glaring at me. "Then we would have had all the proof that we needed."

"What's this? What plan?"

Larry shrugged and looked away, leaving me to explain. I half stuttered while telling Uncle Matt, for he stared at me so intently I was almost afraid that he disapproved of my decision.

"You were right, Kipper," he said when I had finished. "Pretending to drown is pretty serious business, and I could never have allowed that for any reason." He walked to the window. "But, in one way, you were right too, Larry. If we could fool Johanson into thinking we were searching the wall for something else, then he might try to get that money bag out."

"There isn't any other way to do it," Larry grumbled.

"Too bad the breakwall is in such good shape," I said. "If it needed repairs, there'd be a chance that a repairman might stumble on the hiding place."

"Repairs——" Uncle Matt spoke slowly. "We do have the wall checked periodically. There are repairs made every now and then."

"Why not try that, then!" Larry shouted, his anger already gone. "Why not announce that a crew will be coming in to check whether the wall needs repairing under the surface?"

"It's all handled through the car-ferry company," Uncle Matt said. "They're responsible for the upkeep of the wall."

"And they're the ones who want the money and the thief," Larry said. "If you turn the money in and tell them our idea, I'll bet the car-ferry officials will go along with the whole plan."

"The *Wolverine* is in dock tonight," Uncle Matt said. "They're laying in until tomorrow. If this announcement got to Johanson today, he might even try to get to that wall tonight. He'd want to get the money out as fast as he could."

"Can you really get the word out that fast?" I asked.

"I'm going to try." Uncle Matt reached for the money bag and carried it back to the safe. "I think we'll make our plans from here," he said quickly, the uncle gone and the policeman back again. "I'll call Mr. Keever at the car-ferry office and ask him to meet with me here. I don't want any hint that we're plotting anything together. If he agrees to pass the word out today that the wall will be checked within the next few days, I'll guarantee you that our trap will catch Mr. Arnold Johanson hightailing it over there tonight."

He turned to go to the telephone, then he stopped. "Say," he said, turning to us, "I just started to think. You said you searched the breakwall after I left here last night?"

We both started answering at once, but Uncle Matt stopped us cold.

"It was a very foolish thing to do," he said sternly. Then he winked. "But I must admit now that I'm rather glad you did it."

CHAPTER THIRTEEN

Mr. Keever did come to the house, and when he left twenty minutes later, he seemed thirty pounds heavier. He bustled out the door full of excitement and importance, anxious to get back to his office to announce new repair work for the breakwall. The employees of the car-ferry company had their own publications, and he was sure he could get the news to every worker on the boats. Since repair crews from Grand Rapids brought in large boats full of equipment, he said that he could easily have their arrival make front-page news. Any activity in the channel had to be broadcast to all the workers, so the announcement would not seem unusual. Even if the thief were not caught, no damage would be done— the "repair date" would simply be canceled.

"Did you see his eyes when you handed him that bag?" Larry demanded as soon as he had left.

Uncle Matt laughed. "He was surprised, eh?"

"How come you didn't tell him who hid the money, though, Dad? You made it sound as if you wanted everybody on the boats to hear the news because you didn't know who the thief was."

"We haven't proved who the thief is, Larry. We

only suspect that it is Johanson. We hardly even have basis for an accusation."

"He was the one all right," Larry said. "Don't you think so, Kip?"

I paused, wondering whether I should mention my real thoughts. I hated to sound like a wet blanket.

"Well?"

"I keep thinking about the fog man," I said slowly. "I wonder where he fits in."

"Oh, he doesn't fit in at all!" Larry said impatiently. "We just figured things out wrong in the beginning. You think Johanson will try to get the money tonight, Dad?"

"Mr. Keever is planning to announce that the repair crew will arrive in three days—that's the usual notice they give. We can't be sure what Johanson will do. He may decide to leave the money there and hope that the hole won't be discovered. He is off duty tonight, though, since the *Wolverine* is laying in. If he does decide to get the money out, late tonight would be the best time. It's worth a try to wait out there tonight—I'll wait all three nights, if I have to."

"Can we wait with you?" Larry spoke quickly. He stared at his father, waiting. I held my breath.

"It's highly irregular," Uncle Matt said. "Policemen don't usually take two boys along with them on a stakeout."

Larry started to say something more, but Uncle Matt smiled and continued. "But in this case, I think we can arrange something. You boys worked hard enough to deserve to be in on the finale. You'll have to stay out of the way, though. I doubt that there'll be trouble with Johanson, but I don't want to take any foolish chances."

"We'll do everything you say, Dad."

"It may turn out to be a long wait for nothing."

"I don't care. Do you, Kip?"

I shook my head and grinned. "Where'll we wait?"

"That's the best part of this stakeout," Uncle Matt answered. "We can wait in comfort—and you boys can wait in safety. I'll have a couple of my men posted on shore near the beginning of the wall, and the three of us can be hidden out in the lighthouse storeroom at the end of the wall."

"The lighthouse!" Larry's eyes widened.

Uncle Matt nodded. "I figure that if Johanson is our man, he'll get the money out the same way he put it in. He'll be out there in his rowboat."

"And we'll be waiting," Larry said happily.

We were waiting and so was the fog. It drifted in around midnight, blocking out the light of the moon and turning on the wail of the foghorn. We waited until the last car left the beach parking lot, then we hurried out on the wall, glad to be covered by the fog, yet dreading the droning of the foghorn in the lighthouse above our heads.

It was very dark inside the storeroom. All the brightness from the lighthouse was directed to the outside; nothing was used to illuminate the small room at the foot of the stairs. Everything was dirty and dusty. Ropes and boxes covered the floor and a few life preservers leaned against the walls.

I climbed up and sat on one of the stairs in the winding staircase. We left the door open a tiny crack, and when the light on the tower flashed on, I saw the faces of Uncle Matt and Larry; when it flashed off, I saw nothing. It seemed queer to be sitting so silently in the darkness. The foghorn droned steadily. We waited, tense and quiet. The light flashed on, then off; on, then off. The horn blasted, then was silent. I began counting the light flashes.

When there had been more than a hundred signals, I finally heard the sounds we were waiting for. Between the wails of the foghorn I heard rhythmic, muffled noises getting closer and closer. They were too clear, too plain to be waves. In seconds they seemed to pass directly by the lighthouse. I heard an oar strike the wall.

Uncle Matt waited a few moments, then he stepped outside the door, beckoning for us to stay inside. The fog was clearing, and the moon was bright. In a sudden flash from the lighthouse, the whole scene was laid out before us. A man in a rowboat was climbing onto the fishing ledge of the breakwall. Uncle Matt broke into a run. "All right, Arnold!" he shouted. "It's all over now."

I half expected that the figure would jump into the water, or run down the wall—he might have escaped,

for the fog seemed to come and go. But he did nothing. He remained motionless until Uncle Matt
reached him.

CHAPTER FOURTEEN

The four of us walked toward the beach, Larry and I walking several yards behind Uncle Matt and his prisoner. Later Arnold Johanson told Uncle Matt everything, but right then he said nothing. We walked quickly. Suddenly a flashlight glared in our faces.

"What's going on?"

Uncle Matt's beach guards stood in front of us. When they saw Uncle Matt, they lowered their lights. "What happened?"

"We have the thief," Uncle Matt answered.

"The thief! How did h——"

Uncle Matt's voice showed no emotion. "He came in a rowboat. Lew, you go on out now and row the boat back to shore, then drive back to headquarters. Mike, you come with us."

"The money?"

"The company already has it," Uncle Matt answered, and now his voice betrayed some of his happiness. "The case is solved."

You can see how simple the actual robbery was Arnold Johanson was a trusted worker—for years he had been walking in and out of the room where the safe was kept. He couldn't tell Uncle Matt when he had first thought of having a key made—but he knew it had been a long time before he had had the courage to try it out. Uncle Matt had been correct about the wax impression. Johanson had used soft wax to make an impression of the key while right on the ship—it took only a few seconds.

Then, after he had a key made from the impression, he walked around with it, thinking that he'd never do anything with it. He said it just made him feel good to know he had it; he was afraid to try anything more.

He really did have the rowboat for fishing—and he really did use it often. Then, slowly, it dawned on him that perhaps he could use the boat in a plan. Perhaps he could open the safe, clean it out, and be off in his boat before the money was missed. There would be nothing to tie him to the robbery. No one guessed a duplicate key had been made long ago, and the real key was safe in the captain's office.

Johanson had discovered the hole in the breakwall while he was swimming one day, so he had a good hiding place within a few minutes of the shipyard. All he had to do was think of a plausible excuse for having wet clothes. It seemed like such a good setup, and he thought about the money so much, that finally he had to try out his plan.

Of course, when Larry and I found the money inside the wall, the game was up. His long shot had failed. Too many things pointed to Johanson—he had to be the thief.

"Thanks to you boys, the case is solved," Uncle Matt told us later, when we were back in the house. "If you hadn't found that money, though, I'd still be in the dark. Arnold said that he planned to leave the bag in there indefinitely—he only came out tonight because he was afraid the repair crew would find it when they examined the wall."

Larry beamed—his face had been stretched in a huge grin since the moment Johanson had pulled up to the breakwater. He bounced in his chair like a happy puppy. I sat unmoving, wishing I could join in their happiness. I hated to spoil things, but finally I became too uncomfortable to be quiet.

"But what about the fog man?" I asked. "We still haven't figured out where he fits in."

Uncle Matt and Larry stared at each other. I could tell by their looks that they had talked about my strange feelings concerning the eerie old man who prowled their beaches.

Finally it was Larry who broke the silence. "I guess he doesn't fit in at all, Kipper."

"But the food? The beard? The day I saw him walking without limping?"

Uncle Matt cleared his throat. "I don't think the fog man had anything to do with this robbery, Kip. The things you boys found could very easily be explained. That food could have been left in that hut by campers—the beard and even the clothes could have been playthings of some camper's children—we don't know for sure that they even belonged to the fog man. And as for your seeing him walking upright—well, perhaps you were mistaken."

"It was all my fault!" Larry quickly added. "I got all my ideas confused and I convinced you of things that really never existed. Everything we saw was perfectly innocent—we never knew for sure whether the food or even the beard had anything to do with the case."

"But I did see the fog man walking upright," I said.

There was another silence. Then Larry frowned and spoke. "Kipper, you really have a *thing* about that old guy, don't you?"

Maybe he was right, I thought. *Maybe I did have a* thing *about him. Maybe I had built him into such a fantasy that even I was not able to tell where the real and the unreal started or ended.* "Okay," I said, "we won't talk about the fog man anymore."

"Let's talk about our names in the papers!" Larry said.

I laughed—too loudly, perhaps, but I did want to share in their happiness, and sometimes volume makes up for sincerity.

Again I found myself in bed unable to sleep. I felt as though I'd been on a continuous merry-go-round since I'd arrived in Ludington and I was so dizzy that I was sure I would never be able to get off. The music played only one refrain: the fog man, the fog man, the fog man. How easy it is to decide to forget something—and how difficult it is to really do it!

At last, near dawn, I climbed from bed and dressed. As Larry and Uncle Matt slept, I walked from the house and headed toward the lake. I don't know what I really went there for. I don't think I expected to find the answer to the mystery of the fog man. By then I had almost convinced myself that I would never know the truth. Or, I told myself as I walked along, perhaps Larry had been right— perhaps I really did have a *thing* about the old man; perhaps there really was no mystery at all.

I sat on the beach alone. The sun was just beginning to rise; there were only a few sea gulls on the

beach, not a sign of fog. It was so quiet that I heard the sound of the small waves as they washed ashore. I sat there staring at the empty beach, then turned to look at the rising sun. In the distance, I saw a familiar figure walking from the parking lot. I stared, stupefied, as it drew closer. It was Miss Norton coming to open her gift shop. My heart began to beat faster. I swallowed loudly and my lips formed a name. Suddenly I began to run, my footsteps muffled in the soft sand.

She didn't hear me. I ran up behind her, and as she was putting her key in the lock, I spoke. "Fog man!" I said loudly. "Fog man!"

She turned quizzically, as if someone had spoken her name.

CHAPTER FIFTEEN

Her eyes widened when she saw me. "You know?"

I could only stare in answer. The madness that had sent me tearing to her side had left me now and I was as helpless as a bowl of gelatin left in the sun.

"Come in then," she whispered. She opened the door, stepped inside, and pulled me in after her. I felt the crowded shop enclose me like a cocoon.

When the door slammed shut, she hid her face in her hands. She began talking, her words half muffled by her fingers.

"I was afraid you knew," she said. "That first day —here at the beach—I didn't know anyone was near. I was hurrying, almost running, even singing;

then I saw you standing near the wall. I started to limp, but I wasn't sure how much you had seen . . . how much you had heard . . . you looked at me so strangely that I was sure you suspected something."

My head felt dizzy. She was the fog man, then? She? It must have been her walk that had given it away. I must have known all along, subconsciously, that the fog man was neither a man nor a vision, but my conscious mind refused to accept the truth. So she pretended to be an old man. Miss Norton was the fog man . . . but why? Why?

She seemed to grow smaller as she talked. "I didn't know what to do after that robbery that morning," she said, twisting her handkerchief. "I was afraid to go to the beach anymore and I knew the searchers would find that food I'd hidden in the woods. Finally, at dawn, I went out to the hut to bury it. I had to wear my disguise—I'm afraid to walk away from the main road without it. And then you saw me again! I threw away the beard and the clothes and buried the food. I never wanted to see that outfit again!" She put the handkerchief to her face and covered her eyes.

I leaned against the door. How neatly everything fell into place! No wonder the fog man always disappeared from the beach so quickly. Miss Norton's shop was only a few feet away. The back door faced nothing but sand.

"But why did you do it?" I finally said. "Why did you pretend to be a crippled old man?"

"I had to do it! It was all I could think of. This shop was almost bankrupt three years ago. I had to do something to get people to come in here and start buying. I finally decided to make up a mystery; people love mysteries, you know. I bought the old clothes in a second-hand shop in Muskegon, then I bought the beard. When I put on that outfit, I hardly recognized myself."

She looked at the floor and paused. "I guess Larry told you that I'm not very brave. It's true. I was really scared to try out my idea at first, but, finally, I worked up enough courage. And once I tried it, I found it was easy! I felt like a different person when I put on that disguise. I started walking the beach every morning. I made up that story about the old man—I even bought food for *him* to make the story better."

"And you sold his driftwood," I said, pointing to her special display.

"That's what saved my shop," she said quickly. "I sold more driftwood that first summer than I'd sold in the five years I'd been here. People loved to get a piece of driftwood found by the fog man. Even local people bought it."

"And nobody ever recognized you?"

"Never. Most people never came near me. I only walked in the early morning. I told everybody that the old man was a deaf-mute." She shook her head helplessly. "It didn't harm anyone, and it was all so simple."

Simple! I frowned as I remembered the creepy feelings that I had had about the figure of the old man.

"Are you going to tell people?" I heard her ask.

I looked at her again. Her eyes were red, and she stared at me anxiously.

"No," I said. "I won't tell."

She smiled. "What a relief!" Then she looked down. "It's the embarrassment—I'd be so ashamed if anyone knew. Money doesn't worry me now; the shop is all mine finally. I guess there isn't a need for the fog man anymore anyway."

I nodded and backed out of the door. She followed. "Does—does anyone else suspect?"

I paused on the doorstep, remembering how Uncle Matt and Larry had tried to persuade me that I had been wrong about the fog man. "No," I said half smiling. "Nobody else suspects."

Nobody ever did suspect. I stayed in Ludington for a few more days, but everyone was so busy talking about the return of the money and the capture of Arnold Johanson that no one noticed that the fog man was gone. Uncle Matt gave the credit to Larry and me, so the two of us were heroes for awhile. The whole town was full of praise and backslapping.

After I got home, Larry wrote to tell me that the old fellow hadn't been seen since I'd gone—that he finally had left the area for good. I wish I could say that he has left me, too. I can still see him limping, climbing, staring. It's strange that although I know he's not real, I still think about him all the time. I can hardly convince myself that he only lived in imagination in the first place.

I'm sure now that the only way I'll forget him is to find something that will affect me the same way that he did. That first trip to Ludington brought me so many new sensations, and although I know the fog man was only a small part of the whole picture I still connect him to every scene from the summer.

Now, after all this time, Larry has written to ask me whether I would like to spend another week with him.

"We'll just eat, sleep, and fish," he says . . . I wonder. At any rate, I'm going. When I'm back in the home of the fog man, perhaps I'll convince myself that there's nothing more to see, nothing there but a frightened woman trying to sell driftwood. In a way it will be like chasing a dream. I'll chase it until I catch it—then I'll find there is nothing there; unless, of course, I find something else to take its place. But that's too farfetched to worry about now. One adventure like the one I had in Ludington is enough for anybody.

CAROL FARLEY, author of many books for young readers, was born and raised in Ludington, Michigan. Although she has traveled around the world, visiting China and teaching in Seoul, Korea, she says, "My first love is Lake Michigan — all of the people I write about were people I knew in Michigan as I was growing up." She and her husband, who now live in Mt. Pleasant, Michigan, have four children.

Other Avon Camelot Books by
Carol Farley

THE MYSTERY OF THE FIERY MESSAGE
MYSTERY IN THE RAVINE

BOOK ONE

Sir Arthur Conan Doyle's

THE ADVENTURES OF
SHERLOCK HOLMES

Adapted for young readers by Catherine Edwards Sadler

Whose footsteps are those on the stairs of 221-B Baker Street, home of Mr. Sherlock Holmes, the world's greatest detective? And what incredible mysteries will challenge the wits of the genius sleuth this time?

A Study In Scarlet In the first Sherlock Holmes story ever written, Holmes and Watson embark on their first case together—an intriguing murder mystery.
The Red-headed League Holmes comes to the rescue in a most unusual heist!
The Man With The Twisted Lip Is this a case of murder, kidnapping, or something totally unexpected?

Join the uncanny and extraordinary Sherlock Holmes, and his friend and chronicler, Dr. Watson as they tackle dangerous crimes and untangle the most intricate mysteries.

AVON C CAMELOT

AN AVON CAMELOT ORIGINAL • 78089 • $1.95
(ISBN: 0-380-78089-5)

BOOK TWO

Sir Arthur Conan Doyle's

THE ADVENTURES OF
SHERLOCK HOLMES

Adapted for young readers by Catherine Edwards Sadler

The Sign of the Four What starts as a case about a missing person, becomes one of poisonous murder, deceit, and deep intrigue leading to a remote island off the coast of India.

The Adventure of the Blue Carbuncle It's up to Holmes to find the crook when the Countess' diamond is stolen.

The Adventure of the Speckled Band Can Holmes save a young woman from a mysterious death, or will he be too late?

Join the uncanny and extraordinary Sherlock Holmes, and his friend and chronicler, Dr. Watson, as they tackle dangerous crimes and untangle the most intricate mysteries.

AVON CAMELOT

AN AVON CAMELOT ORIGINAL ●78097 ● $1.95
(ISBN: 0-380-78097-6)

BOOK THREE

Sir Arthur Conan Doyle's
THE ADVENTURES OF
SHERLOCK HOLMES

Adapted for young readers by Catherine Edwards Sadler

The Adventure of the Engineer's Thumb When a young engineer arrives in Dr. Watson's office with his thumb missing, it leads to a mystery in a secret mansion, and a ring of deadly criminals.

The Adventure of the Beryl Coronet Holmes is sure that an accused jewel thief is innocent, but will he be able to prove it?

The Adventure of Silver Blaze Where is Silver Blaze, a favored racehorse which has vanished before a big race?

The Adventure of the Musgrave Ritual A family ritual handed down from generation to generation seemed to be mere mumbo-jumbo—until a butler disappears and a house maid goes mad.

Join the uncanny and extraordinary Sherlock Holmes, and his friend and chronicler, Dr. Watson, as they tackle dangerous crimes and untangle the most intricate mysteries.

AVON CAMELOT

BOOK  FOUR

Sir Arthur Conan Doyle's
THE ADVENTURES OF
SHERLOCK HOLMES

Adapted for young readers by Catherine Edwards Sadler

The Adventure of the Reigate Puzzle Holmes comes near death to unravel a devilish case of murder and blackmail.

The Adventure of the Crooked Man The key to this strange mystery lies in the deadly secrets of a wicked man's past.

The Adventure of the Greek Interpreter Sherlock's brilliant older brother joins Holmes on the hunt for a bunch of ruthless villains in a case of kidnapping.

The Adventure of the Naval Treaty Only Holmes can untangle a case that threatens the national security of England, and becomes a matter of life and death.

Join the uncanny and extraordinary Sherlock Holmes, and his friend and chronicler Dr. Watson, as they tackle dangerous crimes and untangle the most intricate mysteries.

AVON CAMELOT

AN AVON CAMELOT ORIGINAL • 78113 • $1.95
(ISBN: 0-380-78113-1)